American ninja!

The gunman was trying to fathom the gloom in the warehouse to confirm that the burst of hail had mowed down the dark figure. Briefly he noted the body of his slain comrade nearby and was surprised and puzzled by the steel star lodged in his skull.

Holding his machine gun bayonet-style, he listened intently. From outside he heard the sounds of the distant firefight, but from within there was only silence. He started to breathe easier. He was safe for the moment.

As he started his cautious retreat, a sound like a rasping sigh made him whirl. He barely had time to take in the hooded figure that had materialized from the shadows with a naked length of steel in his hand.

He registered the hiss of air as the sword was raised overhead for a swift downward stroke, saw only too clearly the glint of cold metal, the burning intent in the eyes above the black mask.

Those were the last things he saw.

Mack Bolan's

PHOENIX FORCE.

PHOENIX FORCE.

GAR WILSON

CHINA COMMAND

A GOLD EAGLE BOOK FROM
W RLDWIDE.

TORONTO · NEW YORK · LONDON · PARIS
AMSTERDAM · STOCKHOLM · HAMBURG
ATHENS · MILAN · TOKYO · SYDNEY

First edition July 1989

ISBN 0-373-61342-3

Special thanks and acknowledgment to
William Fieldhouse for his contribution to this work.

1

George Woodson had often wondered how people in China kept their sanity. He would have thought that a country with a population of more than a billion would be ready to come apart at the seams. But that had been before he arrived in the People's Republic of China. Woodson was from New York City, and he knew what the overcrowded conditions had done to the metropolitan area with a population close to eighteen million. With China's population five times that of the United States, Woodson had figured the Chinese people would have severe problems with keeping everybody fed, and the whole country would be ready for a collective breakdown from being forced to live on top of each other.

However, Woodson was surprised to discover the Chinese were not ready to kill each other for enough space to breathe. The population was incredibly vast, of course, but it was spread across the third largest country in the world, and the overcrowding was far less desperate than what Woodson had seen in Bangladesh and India. As a photojournalist, Woodson had traveled to a lot of countries and seen more suffering, starvation and misery than most Americans could ever imagine. Compared to Delhi and Bombay, Peking and Shanghai were pleasant communities with plenty of elbowroom. In fact the population of Peking—or Beijing as it is more frequently called now—

was less than half that of New York City, and the people were far more polite and agreeable.

Of course the Chinese had centuries of experience with dealing with huge populations. Perhaps the oldest civilization in the world, China had survived wars, famines, foreign domination and political revolutions. The Chinese people had learned to cope with hardships, shortages and overcrowding. Like the Japanese whom Woodson had encountered while stationed in Tokyo before being sent to the People's Republic, the Chinese placed high value on good manners. Crowds pouring into public trains and subways still remained polite. Instead of pushing, jabbing and cursing, the Asians seemed to gently sweep one along with their number, occasionally smiling and nodding in a pleasant gesture of mild apology and understanding greeting.

Woodson recalled the last time he had used a subway in New York. The crowds had been rude, pushy and obnoxious. The cars had been filthy and marked with foul graffiti. His own countrymen seemed barbaric and uncouth compared to the Chinese. The condition of public transportation and the streets in Chinese cities, although less modern and technologically inferior to those in American's, were considerably cleaner and better cared for.

Woodson had been reluctant to accept the assignment to China. He was uncertain about what the country would be like and had reservations about everything from the language barrier to the food and the hazards of being an American in a Communist nation—regardless of the claims of great social changes since the death of Mao. Yet he was glad he had made the trip. It proved to be a delightful and fascinating assignment.

China was full of history—thousands of years of history. The Great Wall, Hangchow, the Imperial Palace, the Temple of Heaven and so much more. There were also such natural attractions as the breathtaking waterfalls at the

Kweichow Mountains and the formidable and awesome Gobi Desert. Yet the greatest appeal to Woodson was the people themselves. The Chinese seemed to be hardworking, generally pleasant and civic-minded. They appeared eager to help the tall American visitor any way they could. A remarkably large number of Chinese spoke English to some degree, and they all wanted to try out their linguistic skills on Woodson.

Unlike the Japanese, the people of China seemed to favor a less hectic pace than most Americans. They haggled over prices, offered special deals on "bargain merchandise," they offered dishes with names Woodson could not pronounce and ingredients he did not really want to find out. Most of all they wanted to know about America and how democracy was working in the United States.

Many young Chinese university students talked about the democratic reforms in China. They liked the changes. Free enterprise offered opportunities Communism could not supply. Most wanted more changes and they wanted them now. They asked Woodson's opinion and advice about how to achieve their goals. The photojournalist was cautious and had no idea what to tell the eager young men in white short-sleeved shirts and neatly pressed dark trousers.

Some of the older Chinese did not appear to be as enthusiastic. Collin Yee, Woodson's interpreter, explained that this had less to do with any animosity felt toward Americans or the notion of democracy than a sense of distrust of politics in general. They recalled too many claims of great changes which never seemed to improve their lives or the lives of their families. The majority of Chinese were concerned more with the needs of their own house than politics. Their first loyalty was to the family.

"What about the stuff I used to hear back in the sixties that every Chinese citizen was supposed to be a representative of Beijing?'' Woodson asked as he followed Yee through the streets of Hangzhou.

"That's what Mao claimed," the interpreter said with a shrug. "Maybe he even believed it, but it never was the truth. The Chinese have always been Chinese, and they always will be. Nothing will change that."

Yee smiled. He was an Eurasian from Hong Kong, and had formerly engaged in covert trade with China. In other words, he was a smuggler and black marketeer. Since besides speaking English, he was fluent in Mandarin and several other dialects, Yee proved an excellent interpreter. He also had contacts in the mainland and soon became a successful guide and translator after Mao's death in 1976. Woodson felt lucky he had hired Yee for his assignment.

They walked past columns of merchants and vendors lined along the streets. More evidence of creeping capitalism in China. A wide variety of curios, food, tea and colas were available. Most of the merchants had acquired some English or at least Pidgin English.

"Lookee one lookee," a grinning old man invited, gesturing at some ugly, ceramic curios on a small table. He sounded like a caricature from an old Hollywood movie set in the Orient. Asian Americans would cringe if they heard him talk. "Nice gifts takee home. Momento of busyness trip. Yes?"

"*Bu shi'eh-shi'eh,*" Collin Yee replied, curtly polite.

The merchant seemed surprised. He probably assumed Woodson and Yee were both American tourists and did not expect either man to speak any Chinese. The man smiled awkwardly and nodded so hard that Woodson would not have been surprised if his head came loose from his neck. Yee led the photojournalist along the pathway to the public gardens.

"You got your camera ready, George?" Yee asked. "This is one of the reasons I brought you to Hangzhou.

Visitors who see only Beijing and the Great Wall miss this attraction. Gardens such as this are an important part of the Chinese culture. When you see it, you will surely understand.''

Yee was right. Woodson realized the value of the Hangzhou gardens the moment he saw the forest of willows and cherry blossom trees. Quaint little bridges spanned quiet ponds. Lily pads floated on the calm waters. Gazebos with graceful pagoda-style rooftops stood on platforms between the bridges. More than a hundred people strolled along the garden path and the ancient network of bridges, yet barely a whisper disturbed the silent, tranquil setting.

George Woodson understood one of the secrets which had helped the Chinese keep their sanity. Places like the Hangzhou garden were shrines to serenity and meditation. The beauty was simple. No huge ornate monuments. No shops, restaurants or lamps with glaring electric lights. Perhaps the gardens were pitch-black at night. Woodson hoped the bridges and footpaths were illuminated with colored lanterns after dark. The site should be caressed in a soft glow rather than exposed to the cruel white blaze of modern floodlights.

The gently swaying willows and hand-hewn bridges and practical shelters created a sense of inner peace and mystery in the garden, making the visitor feel that the mysteries and wonders of life itself seemed to be reflected by the calm and beautiful setting. Woodson raised his Minolta and snapped some shots of the ponds and gazebos though the photographs could not hope to depict the sense of tranquility of the Hangzhou gardens.

Several Western tourists stood at a gazebo and quietly stared at the water. Three were elderly, two white-haired men and a lady with an aluminum walker and glossy silver hair. They were accompanied by a younger couple, a tall dark man who seldom moved his arm from his blond wife's shoulders. Woodson smiled fondly. It was a pleasant sight, which fitted the atmosphere of the gardens.

"Thank you for bringing me here, Collin," Woodson said quietly. "This is a special place."

"I knew you'd understand," Yee replied softly. "Whenever I come to the mainland, I try to spend at least two hours here. It is perhaps the last peaceful place in the world."

Suddenly the insane snarl of automatic weapons erupted from the willows. The explosions of gunshots rattled together in rapid fire to form an enormous roar. Woodson saw the tourists at the gazebo twitch and stumble from the impact of multiple bullets. The old woman collapsed to the platform. Her walker clattered across the walkway as it landed beside her. Blood seeped from her bullet-riddled torso.

"No!" Woodson screamed as he witnessed the obscenity with a sense of horror that rooted him to the spot and forced him to watch, although he wanted to look away.

One of the elderly men fell against a bench. He clawed at the bullets in his chest as he bowed his head and crumpled to his knees. The checkered cloth cap slipped from atop his white locks, and he slid along the length of the bench to end up in a lifeless heap.

The young husband grabbed his wife, embraced her in a desperate bear hug as she screamed in terror and grief. He threw himself to the platform and tried to shield her with his own body while bullets raked the framework of the gazebo. The husband cried out as two slugs crashed into his rib cage and a third shattered his right hip. Still, he held on to his wife in a desperate attempt to protect her from the murderous assault.

The other old man went down as bullets splintered the supports to the ornate roof. He covered his face with both hands, and blood oozed between his trembling fingers. The senior citizen flopped on his back. His heels drummed a short tattoo on the walkway as his body twitched slightly. Then he lay motionless in death, hands still clasped to his bullet-shattered face.

"My God!" Woodson exclaimed as he started to move toward the gazebo.

"No, George!" Yee snapped, seizing the American's elbow. "There's nothing we can do for them!"

Woodson pulled away from Yee's hand, but he froze in place, bitterly aware his companion was right. The young man and his wife were still on the platform of the gazebo, pinned down by another wave of automatic fire. Figures approached from the willows. The gunmen wore dark green coveralls, green caps and scarf-masks around their lower faces. Only their eyes were exposed. Gloved fists clenched short, stocky-looking weapons with wire stocks. Woodson knew almost nothing about firearms, but he realized the killers were armed with submachine guns.

"We've got to get out of here," Yee insisted.

The photojournalist had raised his camera with an automatic, ingrained reflex before he realized he was staring into the viewfinder. He aimed the lens at the assassins and quickly snapped a photo. He swung the Minolta toward the butchered bodies of the slain senior citizens and the helpless young couple who lay waiting to be slaughtered. Bastards, he thought angrily as he snapped another shot of the rapidly approaching gunmen.

"Dammit, George!" Yee exclaimed as he yanked the American's arm. "They'll kill us, too!"

The figures in the viewfinder were getting bigger. The killers were closing in fast. Woodson snapped one more picture and turned toward Yee. The interpreter had already begun to flee across the bridge, away from the attackers. Woodson followed, his heart racing as he heard the chatter of the submachine guns behind him. The woman screamed, and a single pistol shot bellowed in reply. Her screams ended abruptly.

Woodson and Yee ran for the trees at the opposite end of the bridge. It was the only available cover except for the flimsy handrails of the bridge itself. Those were no more apt to stop bullets than the gazebo's framework. Maybe if they could get behind the tree trunks, they could shield themselves from the killers' bullets long enough for the police to arrive.

Oh, Christ! Woodson thought as they bolted across the bridge toward the trees. He recalled seeing a number of uniformed policemen since he arrived in China, but not one of them had carried a gun. What the hell good would the cops do if they showed up? Throw their batons at the gunmen? Blow their whistles and order the creeps with machine guns to throw down their weapons or be reported for gross antisocial behavior. Hell! The police would probably wind up hiding behind the trees along with Woodson and Yee.

Another nagging thought raced through the American's mind in those microseconds as he ran for his life. What the hell was going on? This was Mainland China, not Lebanon or Northern Ireland. Sure, it was a Communist country and Woodson did not expect China to be utopia, but everyone he had met had seemed delighted to have American visitors—or at least they had not been openly hostile. Was this some sort of death squad for the Chinese Secret Service or whatever the hell it was called? Had China and the United States suddenly declared war and Woodson did not know about it?

A figure stepped from behind a tree and moved to the end of the bridge. He wore the same green outfit as the subgun-packing killers, and most of his face, too, was concealed by a scarf-mask. The eyes above the cloth mask were dark, almond-shaped and void of emotion, reptilian eyes, which offered no trace of sympathy or mercy. The man was lean, yet well muscled, with powerful shoulders and a deep chest. He did not carry a submachine gun, although a holstered pistol hung from his right hip. The sinister figure did not touch the gun. His hand rested on the ivory handle of a sword thrust in his gun belt, worn in a cross-draw position.

The sword cleared the scabbard in a single swift motion. Three and a half feet of polished steel flashed in the man's fist. The blade slashed a series of rapid figure eight cuts in the air as the assassin stepped onto the bridge to block the terrified American and his companion.

Collin Yee cried out in alarm and spun about to flee from the swordsman. He collided with Woodson and nearly bowled the photojournalist off his feet. Woodson jumped back, stunned and confused about what to do next. The sword swooped forward and struck Yee from behind. Woodson saw the blade slice through Yee's neck with a single stroke. He saw Yee's head jump from the stump and pitch over the rail to the pond. Blood spurted from the decapitated neck and splashed Woodson's face and shirtfront.

The headless body staggered about briefly as Woodson stared in painful disbelief. The American heard screams from somewhere in the garden. Someone yelled something in Chinese, and a whistle blasted a shrill and useless call. This guy is gonna kill me and the cop acts like this is a stupid basketball game, Woodson thought. He was astonished that he could still think at all as he stared at the ghastly corpse of Collin Yee. His mind was certainly hovering toward the brink of insanity. Too much fear, too much horror. His brain was sure to explode from sheer overload of these terrible sensations.

Yee's knees had buckled and the headless body had collapsed across the bridge. Blood still gushed from the severed arteries in the corpse's neck. The assassin slowly stepped around Yee's body, the sword held in one fist, blade pointed at George Woodson. Crimson stained the steel shaft. Woodson instinctively hurled his camera at the killer's masked face. The sword slashed a fast cross-body stroke and caught the Minolta in midair. The expensive camera exploded from the blow. Plastic and metal hurtled into the sky. The lens popped out and fell into the pond while 35 mm film dropped limply across the twitching corpse of Collin Yee.

Woodson turned to flee. Two of the machinegun-toting killers were positioned at the other end of the bridge. They pointed their weapons upward, as though they were fearful of hitting their sword-swinging comrade. Although the gunmen held their fire, Woodson realized there was no hope of survival by running in their direction. He grabbed the handrail and vaulted over the top, barely thinking of his actions as instinct drove him on.

The American hit the water feet first. The pond was only waist deep, and Woodson's legs and spine were jarred by the sudden impact. He nearly slipped in the muck as he tried to run through the pond. He found that the water weighed down his legs, and he decided to dive, use the water for concealment and try to reach a deeper part of the pond. Maybe, just maybe, there was still a chance to survive.

A terrible pain in his shoulder blades and spine dashed Woodson's hopes as he fell into the water. He was vaguely aware of the chattering report of the killers' submachine guns. The hot projectiles drilled into his body, crushing bone and splitting the spinal cord like a thread. Woodson opened his mouth. Water poured in and funnelled down his throat. He did not even try to resist as the water found its way into his lungs.

However, George Woodson did not drown. A well-placed pistol round crashed into the back of his skull as his body floated along the surface of the pond. The killers on the bridge saw the blood form an inky-looking cloud in the water surrounding the American's corpse. The swordsman nodded his approval to his comrades, and they hurried across the bridge.

2

Yakov Katzenelenbogen placed the Camel cigarette between the trident hooks of the prosthesis attached to the stump of his right arm. The limb had been amputated at the elbow more than two decades ago. It had been damaged beyond repair by an explosion when Katz was an Israeli soldier during the Six Day War, but a thousand battlefields later, Katz was still a warrior.

He did not look like a popular conception of a veteran fighting man, master spy or professional antiterrorist. Yet Katz was all this and more. In his mid-fifties, and slightly overweight, Katz could easily be mistaken for a middle-age college professor who had suffered a nasty accident. His iron-gray hair was short, and his face had a "lived-in" pleasant appearance. Many people had commented that his gentle blue eyes seemed wise and understanding, and his soft-spoken voice sounded cultured and well educated. It was a voice that spoke six languages fluently and several others to a lesser degree. He was knowledgeable in dozens of subjects and could discuss Middle East history or combat strategy with equal ease. Katz was brilliant, worldly and personable. And—when he had to be—he could be very lethal.

The Israeli frowned as he examined the photographs in the file folder Hal Brognola had given him. Katz was the unit commander of Phoenix Force, the best and most unique antiterrorist commando team ever assembled. The file concerned their new mission, and the photos revealed that the situation they would have to deal with was already very ugly indeed.

Hal Brognola leaned back in his chair at the head of the conference table. He was the number one Fed in the United States, the head of the top secret Stony Man operations. Only a handful of people even knew the organization existed, and no one knew all the details about Stony Man except Brognola. The top Fed worked directly for the President and took orders only from the Oval Office. Yet even the President knew little about Stony Man or how it operated. It got results, and that was what mattered. When a situation required the attention of Stony Man operations, it meant all conventional intelligence and military solutions would not work. It was time to throw out the rule book and let Brognola's people run the show.

"Twenty-three victims so far," the Fed explained as he picked up his half-smoked cigar from an ashtray on the table. "The vast majority were American citizens. The rest were Europeans who may or may not have been mistaken for Americans. Most were just tourists, ordinary people who wanted to see the sights of China. The remainder were photojournalists, writers, minor-level sales executives trying to strike up business with Chinese firms. Not a single victim had anything to do with intelligence work of any kind. None of them were politicians or gangsters or anything like that. It's just cold-blooded murder being committed all over China. In Beijing, Shanghai, a lot of other places."

"This has all happened within the last three days?" Gary Manning inquired, glancing over his copy of the report. The big Canadian shook his head sadly. "While we were on our last mission."

"Even Phoenix Force can't be everywhere at once," Brognola stated. "I know all your assignments are tough and the last one was harder than most, but we've got one hell of a mess going on in the People's Republic of China and the President is pretty worried about it.''

"I imagine anybody with family or friends visiting China is getting a little worried, too,'' Rafael Encizo remarked. The Cuban commando had lost most of his family when Castro took control of his island homeland, and many of his friends were killed during the disastrous Bay of Pigs invasion. He felt great empathy for others who suffered similar loss of those close to them.

"Bloody Red China,'' David McCarter snorted. The fox-faced Briton took out a pack of Player's as he spoke. "Another Communist country. Sending us to Czechoslovakia and Yugoslavia to help them deal with terrorism ought to be enough. I can't say I'm terribly thrilled to go on assignment in pinko territory. *Glasnost* or not, the Reds are still the 'other side.' Seems sort of unpatriotic to be pullin' their figurative chestnuts out of the fire.''

"Chestnuts hell,'' Calvin James said, tapping a long finger on his copy of the report. The tall black man rolled his eyes toward the ceiling. "We're talking about American citizens, pal. And other dudes from Western democracies, including a couple from your home stomping ground in England. Those are the folks gettin' killed, not the Chicoms.''

"True,'' Brognola agreed. "But this isn't just a matter of security of Americans abroad—although that's serious enough on its own. Relations with the United States and Mainland China could suffer if this continues. You know, China has been changing a lot since Mao went to the big chop suey shop in the sky.''

"Chop suey was a dish originally concocted by Chinese immigrants in the United States around 1888,'' James commented. "It's not a traditional Chinese dish. I don't know if they serve it in China, let alone in the Hereafter.''

"If chop suey is American, then the Chinese are probably into it by now," the Fed said, shrugging off James's little history lesson and rolling it right into his conversation. "Red China has been adopting more capitalistic principles and leaning steadily toward democracy. Washington is pretty pleased with the way things have been going with the U.S. and China. Everybody would like to keep it that way."

"Whoever killed these people wasn't too concerned about that," Katz commented, gesturing at the photos in his file. "In fact the killers may have entirely different attitudes about China shifting away from Mao's doctrines."

"One thing is for sure," Encizo remarked. "America doesn't need a billion enemies. From what I understand, China really has changed a hell of a lot since Mao died. It's probably more like Yugoslavia than the Soviet Union, and judging from China's willingness to open up trade agreements with countries Mao used to condemn as imperialist oppressors, it looks like China wants to keep that trend going. Hard to say who might disapprove of that. We've seen similar terrorist activity in other countries. More often than not, the finger winds up pointing at Moscow for the root of the troubles."

"Let's not jump to conclusions," Katz urged. "We'll know more when we get there and have a chance to check out the situation for ourselves."

"I'm a little confused about what the hell we're supposed to do when we get there," James admitted. "China is a huge country with over a billion people. They got their own cops, military intelligence, secret service and all that. How are three white guys, one Hispanic and a black dude from the south side of Chicago supposed to do what they can't? I mean, it's not as if we can blend into a crowd unnoticed when we're there."

"The President wants the best people possible on this," Brognola explained. "That's you guys. If nothing else, this will let Beijing know that Washington doesn't blame their government for what's happened."

"Again," Katz began, "we can't jump to conclusions. There's no way we can be certain what the Chinese government may be doing out of the public eye. The Social Affairs Department—SAD—may also have some plans of its own, independent of the National People's Congress or the Party Advisory Commission. China has a very long tradition of espionage and intrigue. Sun Tzu wrote the *Principles of War* sometime around 500 B.C. It was the original handbook for spies and espionage. Intrigue in China hasn't always been the work of the rulers themselves."

"Killing tourists doesn't sound like SAD to me," McCarter commented. "Especially not killing them on the mainland."

"Well, I don't recall that we ever solved a mission by sitting around the War Room talking about it," Manning said with a sigh. "According to the report here, one of the murder victims was decapitated. Apparently he was killed with a sword. That sounds more like TRIO than SAD."

"TRIO is kaput," James reminded his Canadian partner. "All the leaders are dead, and the organization fell apart after we tangled with them in Japan last year."

"Trent helped you with that one, didn't he?" Brognola asked.

"Actually you sent us to Japan because you thought Trent might be working for yakuza gangsters," Katz reminded the Fed. "Instead we came across a TRIO conspiracy, and Trent assisted."

"Yeah, I remember now," Brognola said, consulting another file folder. "Besides being a skilled ninja, Trent also speaks Mandarin Chinese as well as Japanese. He was with you during that mission in Hong Kong in '87. This mission is the sort that Trent might be well suited for. He could be a valuable asset to Phoenix Force in China.''

''Trent's a good man,'' Katz agreed. ''He's always done well with us in the past. We could use him.''

''No argument,'' Encizo added, ''but Trent does have a life of his own. Runs a self-defense school in San Francisco. He may not want to run off to the People's Republic with us.''

''I've known John longer than any of the rest of you,'' James declared. ''He'll do it. The guy's a patriot, and he'll be willing to help just because it's in the best interests of the United States. Besides, he's spent his whole life training to be a ninja warrior. Ever since he was a kid in Japan he's been into martial arts, weapons, training in stealth, camouflage and all that other *ninjutsu* stuff. But John never gets to really be a ninja except when he joins us for a mission. No two ways about it. He'll jump at the chance.''

''Who else will we be working with?'' Manning asked. ''If we can't trust the SAD or the Chinese government, we'll have a lot of trouble trying to accomplish anything in a country nearly the size of Canada with forty times the population.''

''Well, you will be working with SAD,'' the Fed answered. ''Some officials anyway. And CIA people will be working with you, too. The Company doesn't think the Beijing government or SAD are responsible for the murders.''

''That's ducky,'' McCarter muttered. The British ace had risen from his chair and started to pace. McCarter was always filled with nervous energy. He tended to be a bit short-tempered and overanxious before a mission, but in the field he was a superb and highly professional fighting man. ''We all know how infallible the CIA is. Still, I guess we don't have much choice. It seems to be the only game in town.''

"Some town," Manning remarked. "The second-largest Communist nation in the world. All these people are being killed, and we have no idea why. Just a billion suspects."

"What's the matter?" McCarter asked with a wolfish grin. "Don't you like a challenge, mate?"

"You really should get a lobotomy, David," the Canadian replied dryly. "When do we leave?"

"I'm having you flown out to San Francisco to get Trent," Brognola answered. "From there you'll take a special military flight to either Hong Kong or South Korea, whichever we can set up quickly and still maintain security. The next stop after that will be the People's Republic. Customs and all that have been taken care of, and you'll have special government authorization for equipment, firearms and permits to carry. Shouldn't be any problems when you get there."

"If there weren't any problems," Encizo remarked with a slight laugh, "you wouldn't be sending us in the first place."

3

"Huan y'ng," Kuo Chun greeted as she bowed her head in a brief, polite gesture that even she could not dispense with. She had little use for social pleasantries and wasted as little time with them as possible. "Welcome. I am glad to see all of you finally managed to arrive for this meeting."

"We have had considerable duties to attend to, Commander," Ming Ssu replied, annoyed by the woman's rudeness. "You ought to know because you assigned them to us."

Kuo Chun glared at Ming. Her dark brown eyes, flecked with hazel, fixed a hard stare at Ming's round face. She was a hard woman who had led a life of harsh discipline and self-denial. Her face was lined, with stress and bitterness etched into her stern features. Perhaps once she had been attractive, but the years had not worn well on her countenance. Her silver-streaked black hair was short and combed back from her forehead, and the plain style served to emphasize the deep furrows in her brow.

Yet she was only forty-one years old. In contrast to her face, Kuo's body was fit and strong. She exercised daily and watched her diet with care. Kuo did not smoke or drink. She had taken a vow of chastity and never married or indulged in sexual intercourse. The iron virgin regarded things of the flesh as barriers to devotion of mind, spirit and body. She would allow nothing to get in the way of her total commitment to a cause she believed in with all the fiery passion of a fanatic.

That single passion had driven her since she was a young girl in the sixties. She had felt it as she marched with her comrades in the streets of Beijing, with the "Little Red Book" in her fist. So many others had fallen from the path. They had turned against the lessons of glory and denied the supreme wisdom of Chairman Mao. Traitors, Kuo thought. Traitors and weaklings who had surrendered to the enemies of Maoism, seduced by the capitalistic lures of the whore nations of the West.

Kuo Chun had never betrayed the faith. Mao was dead and the Red Guard officially disbanded for more than a decade. Yet no government decree or party-line treachery could dispel what Kuo carried inside her mind and spirit. As long as she lived, the Red Guard still existed, and it would continue to fight the enemies of Chairman Mao— even if those enemies were her own countrymen.

Ming Ssu knew Commander Kuo all too well. He also had been a Red Guard zealot in the sixties. In 1968 he had served in the army and soon became an intelligence officer, and that had led to a career with the Social Affairs Department. He traveled abroad on numerous missions and honed his skills as an espionage agent, propaganda expert, strategist and assassin.

Ming had been involved in an elaborate mission in South Korea, under direct orders from the Central External Liaison Department. It was the biggest operation he had ever handled, and his career seemed about to take off like a rocket. The powerful Liaison Department would certainly promote him to a higher rank in the SAD and greater authority within the organization. However, after Mao died, SAD operations in foreign countries were drastically reduced. Ming was called back to Beijing and reassigned to a drab communications section with no prospects for promotions in the immediate future.

The damage to his personal career had influenced his decision to join Commander Kuo's self-established People's New Guard. Kuo was a natural leader. She delivered fiery speeches and convinced followers to blindly obey her orders as if she were the reincarnation of Mao Tse-tung. Kuo was also a clever strategist in determining targets for a desired political effect on both the opponents and the Chinese masses she hoped to influence. But she knew little about gathering covert intelligence information. She lacked Ming's experience, expertise and connections in the shadowy world of espionage. Kuo needed the former SAD agent, and they both knew it.

"We have decided field operations together," Kuo told Ming as she sat at the head of the teakwood table. "We are comrades, seeking the same goal. Chairman Mao warned that a good Communist does not place personal interests above the interests of the nation and its people. He said it is contemptible for a Communist to seek the limelight instead of working together, with all his energy and spirit, for the good of all."

"Of course, Commander," Ming replied with a nod. He regretted his offensive remarks that had caused Kuo to respond with the short speech, evoking the lessons of Chairman Mao in the process. Ming also realized that the comments about self-interests were verbal barbs aimed at him. Kuo was no fool. She knew why Ming had joined the New Guard.

Feng Teh seemed uncomfortable with Kuo's remarks as well. A tall man, by Chinese standards, Feng was thin and wiry with a ratlike face. The stiff whiskers of his mustache only increased his resemblance to a rodent. He looked like a crook, and one that was best fitted to live in the sewers at that. Although in the final analysis a man can't be judged by his face, Feng Teh was exactly what he appeared to be.

He was the leader of a small but very nasty tong. Feng's Red Fist Society claimed to be descended of the legendary Yellow Turban Society of the Han Dynasty. The Turbans had once been an enormous organization with more than a million members. In fact the Yellow Turbans even dared to defy the Imperial Family in A.D. 168 and launched an unsuccessful insurrection during the reign of Ling Ti. Whether the Red Fist tong was really an off-shoot of these ancient rebels was difficult to prove or deny, but Feng's group had little in common with the ancient Yellow Turban Society.

The Red Fist tong were smugglers, gunrunners and narcotics merchants. They had long been connected with Triad in Thailand and the Golden Triangle opium markets. In 1981 the Red Fist was swallowed up by the Black Serpent tong which was part of TRIO, an international network of Asian criminals which had included Japanese yakuza and Mongolian gangsters of Tosha Khan's New Horde. After TRIO had been virtually destroyed, with its three leaders dead, remnants of the organization drifted into new leadership. Feng had inherited what was left of the Red Fist tong.

Feng had joined the People's New Guard because his tong was not strong enough to stand on its own. The large and powerful Triad Societies would certainly consume or destroy it unless he found some sort of support. The Guard needed financing, weapons and smuggling connections beyond the mainland. The Red Fist Society provided assistance in these matters, and the Guard, in turn, protected Feng and his tong soldiers. Feng Teh's political devotion to Communism was even less than Ming's, but the Guard and the tong needed each other to survive.

"First," Commander Kuo began, placing her palms flat on the table to peer across the table at the four lieutenants under her command. Her back was straight as a steel rod, her head held high, chin above the brim of the high collar of her jacket. "I wish to congratulate Comrade Chien on the success of his raids upon Western barbarians. I salute your dedication, courage and skill, Comrade."

"To serve the people's revolution is a reward unto itself, Comrade Commander," Chien stated with a deep bow. "I thank you for your praise, yet we all fight the same battles—be it with words or weapons."

Chien was younger than the others. At twenty-five, he still felt the fierce idealism of a young zealot with limited experience to challenge his beliefs. Chien was in his physical prime and had the strength and endurance of youth. He had trained since childhood in various martial arts and served with a paratrooper division in the People's Army. Chien was a killer, a living machine of mayhem, driven by extremist ideas and willing to carry out any orders for destruction without question.

Ming and Feng both found Chien to be disturbing company. The young assassin frequently carried a double-edged sword as well as a pistol holstered on his hip. He favored the sword and would rather kill with the blade than a bullet because it allowed him to feel the life seep from an opponent. Chien also claimed that he could feel the life of a victim travel through the steel in his hand and sink into his own flesh. He felt killing made him stronger. The more life he took, the more he received.

Chien's superbly fit body and handsome young features would have made him a very appealing fellow for the ladies, but he had little interest in women. He had taken a vow to abstain from sex and other pleasures until China had won its "second revolution." Besides, his manner robbed him of his physical appeal, and most women found him too aloof, too cold or just plain frightening.

Commander Kuo thought Chien was a perfect example of a dedicated soldier of the revolution. Of course she and Chien had much in common. Kuo glanced at the painting of Chairman Mao on the wall. The Chairman would be proud of Chien, she thought. And he would be proud of me and what we shall accomplish in his name.

"In his wisdom," Kuo began with a slight smile, "Chairman Mao once said that speeches and resolutions should be concise and brief, and meetings should not go on too long—an arrangement, which will certainly please everyone in this room. So let us get to the point and make this meeting as brief as possible. Thanks to the success of Comrade Chien and his Mao Commandos, we are ready to take this operation to its next phase."

"Commander," Ming began, "I must disagree. Taking this campaign to the next phase too quickly could endanger our entire operation."

"Any thinking that relaxes the will to fight is wrong," Kuo announced, reciting the passage as if it were gospel.

"Actually, Mao said, 'thinking that relaxes the will to fight *and* belittles the enemy is wrong,'" Ming corrected, unable to repress a smile of satisfaction. "I am trying to warn you about the risk of belittling our enemies. As long as you're going to insist on quoting Mao every other minute, may I also remind you that he also warned commanders to pay attention to comrades with opinions that differ from their own."

"Very well," Kuo said with a stiff nod. "I am listening."

"A large number of Americans and Western Europeans have been killed," Ming stated. "That's fine, but it also means the American CIA has certainly started an investigation. So has our own country's SAD, as well as local police and militia forces. Perhaps British SIS, West German BND or the French Sûreté are also trying to hunt us down. There are too many imperialist forces and their running dog lackeys for us. To act now could leave us open to discovery."

Kuo's eyes hardened, although she was secretly amused by Ming's use of trite Party clichés. "Imperialist forces," and "running dog lackeys" were expressions commonly used by the ex-SAD agent. He had obviously used the terms to appeal to the more zealous members of the New Guard— including Kuo. However, she could not dismiss his arguments because he was trying to play silly word games to give the impression he was really one of them. Kuo considered herself to be a dedicated revolutionary, and Ming had not joined them because he believed in their cause. He was not one of them, but that was exactly why Ming was so valuable.

"Your point is taken, Comrade," Kuo assured him. "However, the next phase will be very different from the first. Different targets, different personnel carrying out the attacks. You have been working with Comrade Feng to prepare those American thugs?"

"Yes," Ming confirmed, "but I'm not convinced they're ready. Besides, only two of them are Americans. The others are Europeans. At any rate, none of them can be trusted."

"No occidentals can be trusted," Chien declared firmly.

"Well, the men we'll be working with certainly can't be called reliable. Gowers and Kelly are American deserters from the Vietnam conflict. They joined opium Triad in Laos and later moved to Thailand where they eventually became transporters for my Red Fist tong. They ran into a bit of trouble in Thailand, and they've been looking for a new place to roost. The pair have followed orders and done as they were told in the past, but we must always remember they are greedy, amoral and apolitical. They have turned against the United States, but they are not good communists. We cannot trust their loyalty to our cause. They are loyal only to their own best interests. For now their best interests are to follow our orders and survive."

"The Europeans aren't much more reliable," Ming added. "Neville, the Englishman, is more or less the leader of their group. Most are former mercenaries who violated their governments' laws and can't return home unless they wish to go to prison. Then there are smugglers, mostly from Singapore or Hong Kong. They're criminals and hired killers, not espionage agents or commandos. Of course Neville and some of the others are experienced soldiers. So are the two American traitors."

"Traitors?" Kuo frowned. "You mean defectors."

"They deserted because they were involved in black market drugs with gangsters in Saigon," Ming answered. "The army would have sent them to prison. That's why they 'defected.' It had nothing to do with politics."

"I am aware of their background, and I realize they may be less than perfect allies," Commander Kuo stated. "However, we are unrealistic to expect to find perfection among the occidentals willing to assist us. Caucasians are dishonorable and corrupt by nature. The Russians were supposed to be our allies, and we learned they could not be trusted, either. More time will not make the deserters and mercenaries more honorable. You will simply have to control them."

"I didn't say it would be impossible," Ming stated with a weary sigh. "I simply said I think we need more time."

"We Chinese have always been patient," Kuo declared. "We take pride in our ability to endure hardships and shortages, to make the best of bad situations and make a little go far enough to meet many needs. These are admirable traits, but there are times when waiting is a weakness, which will leave us more vulnerable than action. At the risk of annoying Comrade Ming, I remind you what Chairman Mao said about our style of combat as revolutionary warriors. Fighting is to be continuous, with successive battles fought in short time periods with little rest. If we rest, the enemy too will rest."

"They can afford to rest," Ming muttered. "There are millions of them and only a few of us."

"Chairman Mao warned us to rid our ranks of impotent thinking," Chien declared, his eyes ablaze with the glee of a fanatic quoting the scriptures of his god. "He described this as 'views that overestimate the strength of the enemy and underestimate the strength of the people.' Your thinking is dangerously close to being impotent, Comrade."

What makes you so certain we represent the people, you brainwashed idiot? Ming thought, but he knew better than to express such notions, especially when Chien might respond with his sword if angered by Ming's observation. Before the former intelligence officer could utter a less hazardous answer to Chien's statement, Commander Kuo spoke up.

"Comrade Chien, your passion for the revolution is admirable," she declared quickly, "but Comrade Ming is as concerned as we are with success and the victory of our mission. I value his advice, although I may not always choose to follow it. We shall move to the next phase of our operation. Comrade Lin?"

Lin No-su seemed startled when Commander Kuo spoke his name. The fourth and—although none of the lieutenants under Kuo had any official title—the lowest ranking member of the self-styled rebel leaders, he seldom spoke, and the others rarely asked his opinion or advice. Lin was a short, portly man who always seemed on the brink of a nervous breakdown. A former sergeant in the army corps of engineers, his main expertise was explosives, demolitions and maintenance of weapons.

"Shi," Lin said with a nervous nod. "Yes, Commander?"

"The explosives and weapons are ready?" Kuo inquired. "Are they not?"

"Of course," Lin confirmed. "Comrade Feng's sources managed to get more than a dozen American-made M-16 assault rifles. The weapons were purchased through black market sources in Southeast Asia."

"The Americans left thousands of M-16 rifles in Vietnam when they pulled out," Feng explained. "Many other weapons, as well: M-60 machine guns, Colt pistols, even some tanks and helicopters."

"That's fascinating, Comrade," Kuo said with a slight sigh. She did not give a damn where the weapons came from as long as they fit the needs of their plan. "You are certain of the ammunition as well as the weapons, Comrade?"

"Absolutely," Lin answered, bobbing his head like an idiot. "All American-made 5.56 millimeter. The explosives are Composition-Three, a military plastic explosive used by American soldiers."

"If all the weapons and equipment are in proper working order and the Caucasians are ready for their role in the mission," Commander Kuo stated, "then I see no reason to delay. Comrade Ming, you and Comrade Chien will supervise the troops. Feng, make certain our allies understand what is expected of them. They should also be reminded that any effort to betray us or to fail to carry out their part of the mission won't be tolerated."

"Don't worry, Comrade Commander," Feng assured her. "The two Americans have seen my tong enforcers deal with traitors in the past. They witnessed the mutilation and torture suffered by enemies of my Red Fist Society. Surely they have told the others what fate awaits those who would betray us. I'm certain they also know how the Red Guard has dealt with enemies of the state in the past and that we would not hesitate to do so again."

"It would give me great pleasure to cause any white scum agony," Chien said with a dreamlike glaze in his eyes.

"Many will suffer before this is over," Commander Kuo stated as she gazed up at the painting of Mao Tse-tung. "The enemies of the people's revolution will suffer and die. Chinese or foreign devils of the imperialist West, all will die."

4

Calvin James tried to push open the door to the Kaiju American-Japanese School of Self Defense, although a sign in the window declared the place was closed. Yakov Katzenelenbogen stood at the foot of the stairs, shaking his head slightly as he took a pack of Camels from a jacket pocket.

"I can't believe John isn't here," James remarked with a helpless shrug. "He can't be found at home and he's not here. I guess we have to go to Inoshiro's TV repair shop and see if John's hangin' out with his uncle."

"Trent may not be there," Katz replied, lighting a cigarette with his battered old Ronson. "After all, the man might have some other personal interests besides his *dojo* and his uncle."

"You mean a girlfriend or something?" James asked, slightly surprised by the idea.

"Why wouldn't Trent have a girlfriend?" the Israeli said with a slight smile. "I realize this is San Francisco..."

"I used to be a cop in this city," the black commando said dryly. "Not everybody in San Francisco is lookin' for a gay old time. I never thought to ask John if he had a girl in town. He's not the sort to volunteer information like that."

"He's never seemed to be one for small talk," Katz agreed. The Phoenix Force commander watched a cable car roll along the street. It was crammed with passengers. Cable cars were a big attraction in Frisco. Katz did not understand why. The idea of being jammed into a primitive electric vehicle with forty or fifty strangers did not appeal to the Israeli.

"I sure wish I'd asked him a few details about what the hell he's been doing besides running this damn school," James confessed, descending the stairs to stand beside the Israeli.

"We didn't have much time to discuss anything but the mission when we last worked with Trent in Japan," Katz replied.

He watched the cable car climb up a hill. It reminded him of a sardine can pulled by an electric track. All those people. Unexpectedly a chill shot up the Israeli's back. He suddenly realized why the cable car disturbed him. It reminded him of a cattle car loaded with people. That was an image no Jew who had survived the Nazi regime in Europe would ever forget.

"Yakov?" James asked, puzzled by the strange sadness in the older man's expression. "Something wrong, man?"

"No," Katz assured him, looking away from the cable car. "Not really. I was just letting my mind wander in directions I should avoid. Things from the past."

"Well, this is a city that makes you think about the past sometimes." James gazed at the surrounding buildings. "Lots of history in Frisco."

There were buildings that had survived the great earthquake of 1906. Many had ornate balconies and old fire escapes. Some reflected the charm of turn of the century style, and others were modern, efficient and generally ugly. A blanket of smog hovered over the city. The Golden Gate Bridge was out there somewhere, but it was not visible beyond the fog of man-made grime.

"We'd better find this Inoshiro character and see if he knows where Trent is—" Katz began.

Glass shattered, and an unexpected shrill scream mixed with the abrasive violent sound. A large windowpane to a coffee shop had burst apart as a young man's body hurtled through the glass. He fell to the sidewalk, blood oozing from numerous cuts. Another man, young with shoulder-length blond hair, appeared at the door. His face was contorted with fear and desperation. He suddenly pitched forward to the pavement.

"You ain't goin' nowhere, faggot!" a voice snarled from within the coffee shop.

A man stepped from the doorway. He was young, but his shaved head made it difficult to guess his age. He could have been eighteen or thirty. The vicious sneer on his lips seemed to suit his style of clothing. He wore a denim shirt with the sleeves cut off to display an array of tattoos on his arms. Swastikas and SS rune marks decorated his tattered garments. The cuffs of his Levi's trousers were stuffed inside a pair of English work boots. A length of chain was wrapped around his gloved fist.

Another youth climbed through the broken window. His appearance and style of dress resembled the first punk, with shaved head, boots, and neo-Nazi ornaments clipped to army surplus flight jacket. His weapon was a short black billy club in his fist. Both men attacked the fallen figures. They lashed vicious kicks into the helpless men on the sidewalk. A third hoodlum emerged from the doorway. He sported a large black swastika on his white T-shirt. Like the others, his head was shaved and his face glowed with sadistic glee as he watched his friends assault the two fallen victims.

"Goddamn skinheads," Calvin James hissed as he galloped across the street.

Katz followed his younger partner. He had heard about skinheads, seen news reports on television about the radical, often violent youth movement, but he had never seen them before. Perhaps he had, in Europe in the 1930s and '40s when bullies of the Hitler Youth Movement attacked anyone and anything contrary to the views of the Third Reich.

Skinheads were ready to protest anything, Katz knew, and that included being violently antiblack and anti-Semitic, and detesting foreigners. Not all skinheads participated in such behavior. Some were a variation of the punk rockers of the '70s; but others—bigoted, destructive, murderous bands of vicious young toughs—were the breed that had rightly alarmed the American public. There was no doubt that the three skinheads in the coffee shop belonged to that category.

"Help! Please!" a voice called weakly from inside the shop. The plea was terminated by the sound of a fist striking flesh.

"Hey!" the creep in the Nazi T-shirt cried out as he saw James and Katz approach. "We got company, man!"

The two skinheads who had been kicking the injured men in the street stopped their attack and turned to face the Phoenix pair. The hood with the chain slowly unwound his weapon from his fist. The other skinhead smiled at James and Katz as he tapped the billy club on his open palm.

"You fuckers should have stayed out of this," the guy in the swastika shirt remarked as he leaned on the doorway and looked at the approaching Phoenix commandos with amusement.

The pair did not seem very threatening to the skinheads. James was tall and athletic, although the loose-fitting blue suit he wore made it difficult to judge his physique. They figured the black guy might give them a little trouble, but the older man would be candy. Middle-aged, a bit soft around the waist, and the old goat had an artificial arm to boot. What a pair of idiots.

"Hey, this coffee shop is run by a goddamn kike," the brute with the chain announced as if justifying their actions. "We found these queers inside the joint, so we figured we'd teach them a lesson along with the Christ-killer."

"Looks like we'll have to teach this uppity nigger some manners, too," the club-wielding goon remarked. "Shouldn't put your ugly flat ape nose in the business of white men."

"Who's your buddy, Sambo?" the swastika-lover in the doorway inquired. "Your sweetie?"

"Yeah," the chain-man giggled. "A one-armed, over-aged queen with his spade stud."

"Actually, I'm one of those kikes you fellas like to beat up," Katz told him in a calm voice. "You want to try me, boy?"

"Shit—" the skinhead with the chain snorted and suddenly lashed out with the steel links in his fist.

Katz raised his prosthesis. The chain struck the artificial limb and wrapped around the metal arm. Katz clamped the trident hooks around the links and held the chain firmly and grabbed it with his left hand. He pulled hard. The startled hoodlum stumbled forward, surprised by the Israeli's strength. Katz lashed out a front-kick and slammed the toe of his shoe into the skinhead's groin.

The thug doubled up in agony. Katz hammered the bottom of his fist into the collarbone and whipped up his prosthesis to smash the steel hooks and the chain into the skinhead's face. The youth's head snapped back from the blow, and blood trickled from his torn lips and broken nose. Katz nailed him with his left fist and the skinhead fell unconscious to the pavement.

The club-wielding thug had attacked Calvin James a split second after his companion launched his clumsy assault on Katz. The black warrior raised his arms as if to protect himself from the skinhead's cudgel. The motion drew the attacker's attention, and he did not see the karate side-kick, which crashed into his left kneecap. Bone and cartilage crunched. The hood gasped in pain and swung a wild club stroke at James even as his leg folded up under him.

The billy missed and the skinhead tried a hard-swinging backhand stroke. The black man's hands chopped like ebony ax blades across the skinhead's forearm. The blow jarred the ulnar nerve and knocked the club from the attacker's grasp. James quickly rammed a knee into his opponent's abdomen, making him groan and bend over, nearly vomiting from the blow. James raised a hand to strike once more, but he glimpsed the skinhead at the doorway reaching for something at the small of his back.

James grabbed his stunned opponent and shoved him at the one with the Nazi shirt. The Phoenix pro used the limp skinhead as a battering ram, driving the guy's shaved head into the belly of the slob at the door. The swastika boy moaned breathlessly as the wind was driven from his lungs. He still managed to draw a German Luger from under his shirt, but he did not manage to aim or fire. James did not give him a second chance. A well-placed snap-kick to the wrist sent the Luger hurtling from the skinhead's hand.

The black warrior drove both opponents through the doorway, into the coffee shop. His fists lashed out. One hammered the doubled up skinhead between the shoulder blades and then dropped him face down onto the floor. The other blow crashed into the side of Nazi-Shirt's jaw. Staggering across the room, the stunned man fell against a table with a checkered cloth, a small vase and two cooling cups of coffee.

James stamped the heel of his foot into the back of the fallen man's neck to make certain he did not rejoin the fight. Movement near the window drew the Phoenix commando's attention. A fourth skinhead stood by the broken windowpane, a .38 revolver in his fist. James stood still and raised his arms as the gunman pointed his weapon.

"Now I get to kill me a nigger!" the skinhead said with a nervous laugh as he cocked the revolver.

A chain whistled through the smashed windowpane and struck the gunman's wrists. The impact drove the man's hands downward, and the revolver barked. A .38 slug burrowed harmlessly into the floorboards. Yakov Katzenelenbogen leaped through the window and dived against the startled skinhead. The hooks of his prosthesis struck the gun from the man's fingers, and the force of his lunge drove him backward. Both Katz and the youth stumbled into a table and two chairs, jamming the edge of the table into a wall and sending a chair clattering to the floor.

As Katz shoved the skinhead across the tabletop, the steel claws of his prosthesis raked across the hood's chest. Fabric tore, and the hooks ripped into flesh beneath the man's shirt. He cried out and tried to rise. Katz slammed his fist into the thug's face and knocked him back to the table. The Israeli raised his right arm and bent his elbow, the prosthesis cocked back to his ear, and delivered a powerful downward elbow smash to his opponent's solar plexus. The man's body convulsed in breathless agony.

The Phoenix Force commander yanked his opponent off the table and allowed him to crash to the floor. The proud owner of the swastika shirt had recovered from the blows he had received and attacked Calvin James with a chair. He swung the furniture at the black war machine, but the chair proved an awkward club. James dodged the clumsy attack and launched a powerful side-kick into the backrest of the chair. The kick sent the chair flying while the hood hurtled across the room into a counter. The thug fell against a trio of large metal coffee urns. His arm hit a nozzle to one urn, and a stream of steaming fresh coffee poured down to the floor.

James closed in and whipped the back of his fist across the skinhead's face. He followed with a hard karate chop under the heart. The hood folded with a groan, and James grabbed the punk's left ear and shoved his head against an urn. There was a clanging sound, then James drove an uppercut under his opponent's breastbone.

"You guys oughta call yourselves 'shitheads,'" James hissed as he followed up with a blow to the point of the hoodlum's jaw. There was no more argument.

Katz had also finished off his opponent with a kick behind the ear. The Phoenix pair exchanged nods to confirm that they were unharmed. Just then a figure slowly rose from behind the counter. A middle-aged man with a bruised mouth and a pair of broken glasses perched on his nose peered at the commandos with disbelief.

"Thank God you came," he said with a sigh of relief. "They were gonna kill me. Those bastards attacked two boys who were just sitting there drinking coffee."

"Did you call the police?" James asked as he turned off the coffee urn. "And the ambulance. The guy who went through the window got cut up, and the other fellow could have a fractured skull. I don't know if anybody gives a damn about the skinheads, but none of them are gonna die. But they won't be up to causing any trouble for a while."

"Uh, I'll call now," the shop owner declared. "I don't know how to thank you."

"No need to thank us," Katz assured him, gathering up the fallen .38 revolver. "At least our trip here hasn't been a total waste. Do you know how to use this?"

"A gun?" The man shook his head. "Of course not. I'm an honest, law-abiding person."

"That's sometimes the sort who should learn to handle a gun," Katz commented. "These fellows might wake up. If they do, you may have to use this. Don't even touch it otherwise."

"Here's another one," James added as he placed the Luger on the counter. "Pretty good chance they'll take off if you just threaten them with a gun. If they come at you, point the gun at the chest of the closest bastard and squeeze the trigger."

"Oh, God," the shop owner said, staring at the handguns as if they were a pair of king cobras. "I don't know if I can do that. Won't you gentlemen stay?"

"Sorry, we have to go," Katz replied. "Don't forget to make those phone calls."

"Good luck," James told the guy, and headed for the door.

Katz followed his partner from the shop. James stepped over the senseless skinhead on the pavement and knelt by the fellow who had been heaved through the window. The man was semiconscious, and the bleeding did not seem too serious. He looked up at James with blurry eyes.

"You'll be okay," James told him. "Just lie still and wait for the ambulance to arrive."

The man weakly nodded in reply. James moved to the other victim, finding him dazed, the back of his head bloodstained. He held a hand to his side and groaned slightly. Broken rib, James thought.

"We've got to go," Katz reminded his companion.

"I know," James agreed and started to rise. He was a former SEAL corpsman in the navy and currently the unit medic for Phoenix Force. He was reluctant to leave the injured victims of senseless violence.

A battered old pickup truck suddenly pulled up to the curb. Two young men with shaved heads rode in the back of the vehicle. One of them pointed a .357 Magnum revolver at the Phoenix pair. The truck came to a halt and a third skinhead swung open the door at the passenger side. He held a sawed-off shotgun in his fists. James and Katz stared at the twin muzzles of the scattergun and slowly raised their hands.

"Don't move, you fuckers!" the shotgunner ordered.

"Don't worry," James muttered. Few things were more disturbing than staring into the muzzles of a double-barrel shotgun.

The door opened on the driver's side, and a fourth youth stomped around the front of the truck. The two hoodlums in the back of the vehicle climbed down to the sidewalk, while the skinhead with the .357 kept his weapon aimed at the two Phoenix commandos. His partner carried a tire iron in his fist.

The skinheads looked remarkably alike. They were all roughly the same age, similar in height and build. All wore the thrown-together "uniform" of a skinhead. The shaved heads, twisted arrogant sneers and eyes ablaze with unreasoning hatred seemed identical on each man's face. They could have been clones, produced from a secret stronghold run by a mad scientist.

"What the hell did you bastards do to our brothers?" the driver demanded, fondling the handle of a large Bowie knife on his belt.

"Well, we were strolling along and saw these guys lying around out here," James began. "Somebody beat 'em up, and we thought they might need a Band-Aid or something."

"Shut up, nigger!" the shotgun man snapped, his weapon pointed at James's stomach. The skinhead stepped from the truck and looked James up and down as if examining a diseased leper. "I never met a spear-chucker yet who told the truth."

"When you point one of those things at somebody," the black commando replied, "expect him to try to say anything that'll stop you from pulling the trigger."

"You were told to shut up, boy," the driver hissed, drawing his knife. "Maybe I'll cut your tongue out to teach you a lesson."

"Do you people have a point, or are you just fond of mindless violence and bullying people for amusement?" Katz inquired, lowering his arms slightly.

"You assholes are gonna be real sorry you messed with us," the shotgun man declared.

The skinhead with the revolver suddenly cried out in unexpected pain as a hand chopped across his wrist. The revolver fell to the pavement. A tall, slender man dressed in a black karate *gi* uniform stood behind the gunman. He had crept silently behind the skinheads and they hadn't known he was there until he'd struck.

The hood glimpsed the man's face, a combination of Caucasian and Asian features. The dark almond eyes met those of the skinhead for a fragment of a second before a heel-of-the-palm stroke slammed under the young thug's jaw. The blow knocked him back into the frame of the truck as the skinhead with the tire iron turned toward the figure in black.

John Trent held his hands ready, fingers clawed like an eagle about to attack. The skinhead glanced at the karate outfit and snickered. That Jap crap wouldn't do any good against a tire iron, he figured. Trent saw the contempt in his opponent's face. Only a fool underestimates an opponent, and the skinhead was obviously a fool.

Trent snapped a slipper-clad foot forward. The hood swung his iron to try to block the kick, determined to shatter Trent's shinbone with a single blow. However, the kick was a feint. Trent's other leg executed the real attack. His foot slammed into the goon's forearm above the elbow. The shock to the ulnar nerve sent a violent quiver through the skinhead's arm, and the tire iron fell from trembling fingers.

The iron clattered on the sidewalk. Trent's fist shot forward in a ram's-head punch, knuckles crashing into the skinhead's jaw. The thug was jarred violently by the punch, and Trent quickly grabbed the man's tattered jacket and pumped a knee between his legs. The skinhead gasped and wheezed in agony. Trent held on to the jacket, jammed a hip into his opponent's stomach and hurled him over the hip to send him sailing into the thug who had formerly packed the .357 Mag.

Calvin James instantly took advantage of the situation. The shotgun man was distracted by Trent's attack on two of his companions. James quickly swung a palm under the barrels of his opponent's weapon and pushed the shotgun toward the sky. The blaster roared, and a burst of buckshot exploded harmlessly overhead.

James reached inside his jacket with his left hand while with the right he held onto the shotgun. He drew a Jet Aer G-96 fighting dagger from its sheath under his right arm, and with a flash of steel, the five-inch steel blade slashed the gunman's fist. The sharp edge sliced the back of the skinhead's hand. He cried out and lost his grip on the shotgun. James still held the barrels in his right fist. He slammed the shotgun into the face of its owner. The thug fell back against the door of the truck, blood flowing from a mashed-in nose.

The black warrior's left hand struck again. He hammered the butt of his dagger into the dome of the hoodlum's shaved skull. The skinhead uttered a slight moan and slumped unconscious at James's feet. The Phoenix pro turned toward the two men Trent had jumped. One was already sprawled senseless on the sidewalk. Trent had the other creep pinned against the side of the truck and smashed him under the jaw with an *empi* stroke. Trent's elbow struck hard, and his arm rose with the motion to swiftly deliver a karate chop across the side of his opponent's neck. Another skinhead fell limply to the pavement.

Katz stepped back from the fourth and final skinhead. He reached inside his jacket and pulled a SIG-Sauer P-226 pistol from shoulder leather. The astonished skinhead stared at the gun with disbelief as the Israeli pointed it at his face.

"I'm getting very tired of you morons," Katz announced. "Turn around, put your hands on the hood of the truck. Spread-eagle."

"Sure, sure," the punk replied fearfully. He dropped his knife and turned slowly to the truck. "Whatever you say. Uh, you fellas cops?"

The skinhead put his hands on the truck and spread his legs shoulder-width apart. Katz stepped behind the young hood and chopped the butt of his pistol behind his ear. The man fell across the hood and slid unconscious to the sidewalk. Katz returned his SIG-Sauer autoloader to the holster under his jacket and turned toward Calvin James and John Trent.

"You showed up at a very apt moment, John," Katz remarked. "Where did you come from?"

"I was in my office in the school across the street," Trent explained. "I heard a gunshot and glass break. I looked outside and saw you two. Then these four lower animal life-forms arrived in the truck."

"Glad you gave us a hand with them," James admitted. "There are four more of these baldheaded cockroaches inside the shop. Well, one is lying out here. You got many skinheads in San Francisco these days?"

"Too many," Trent answered. "But less than some other cities, I suppose. These maggots are probably from Los Angeles. They come up here sometimes. Usually to try to find gays—or at least someone they *think* is gay—and beat them up. Are you looking for me, or did you just happen to be in the area?"

"We need to talk," Katz declared.

5

The yellow Toyota headed for Fisherman's Wharf. Dozens of restaurants, curio shops and odd specialty museums were located in the area. The wharf was a popular, colorful section of San Francisco. Calvin James drove the rented Toyota to the wharf to take advantage of the traffic and crowds. After the incident at the coffee shop, James and Katz wanted to avoid the police. They could not afford to be tied up with questions about their encounter with the skinheads. The best place to conceal a car is among a lot of other cars. The best place to avoid drawing attention is to be in a place where everyone is busy with interests of their own.

"Hey, John," the black man began as he drove the rental in circles, trying to find a parking space. "If you were in your office, how come the *dojo* was closed?"

"I was going through my files," Trent answered. He sat in the back seat, glancing at the windows with little interest. "The school is closed because I'm not certain I'll be able to run it much longer. I may have to sell it."

"Why?" James asked, surprised that Trent was having business problems. "I always thought your school did pretty well."

"Interest in martial arts isn't as great as it was a few years ago," Trent answered. "Then I had to close the *dojo* for a month last year when I made that trip to Japan. A number of new students decided to go to a different school. I can't blame them for that. Some of my other students have moved from the city for various reasons. A couple of teenagers joined the Armed Forces. Others went to college or left San Francisco to try to find jobs elsewhere. All these factors have caused problems. Then, the Internal Revenue Service contacted me on the first of this month."

"An audit?" Yakov Katzenelenbogen asked. He sat in the front seat next to James. "Any particular reason?"

"Income tax is one of those man-made mysteries I shall never understand," Trent replied with a sigh. "Being self-employed and single causes quite a few problems. It limits one's deductions, requires higher social security payments—a lot of other things I don't understand. All I know is if they have another 'tax reform,' I may just commit seppuku before the IRS does it for me."

James frowned. Trent was half-Japanese, on his mother's side. He was not apt to make remarks about seppuku lightly. Seppuku is a form of ritual suicide by disembowelment, often referred to incorrectly as "hari-kari" by Westerners. James had actually seen a man commit seppuku right before his eyes. It was a horrible sight he would never forget and hoped never to witness again. The idea that his friend might seriously consider that option made James very uncomfortable.

Strange what frightens individuals, James thought. Trent was fearless in combat. The American ninja wouldn't hesitate to charge into battle against three or four armed opponents, yet the tax audit had obviously upset him. Maybe because it was an opponent he could not fight with a sword or a gun.

"Apparently the IRS was also curious about my income over the past three years," Trent continued. "Whatever branch of the government you fellows work for paid me about a year's income for each mission I assisted you with in the past. That was greatly appreciated, and I don't wish to complain, but the confirmation that I earned this money legally, doing some sort of confidential work for the military or whatever, did not materialize. Thus, I have no proof for my increased income for two years or the sudden drop in income for the last year. The IRS is asking a lot of questions, and I don't know how to answer them.''

"And you didn't know how to contact us to get the situation straightened out," Katz said with a nod. "We'll get in touch with our control officer and have everything taken care of, John. There was obviously a failure of someone to make the proper arrangements and cut through the red tape."

"Don't worry, man," James urged. "The IRS will be off your back. Speaking of income, you might be interested in making another year's wages, provided you live to collect it."

"You came to recruit me for another mission?" Trent raised his eyebrows with interest. "Very well. I accept."

"Perhaps you should hear it first," Katz suggested.

"I don't need to," Trent replied. "I'll welcome a chance to fight *anyone* if it means I don't have to fight the IRS. Where will we be going?"

"The People's Republic of China," Katz answered. "Have you ever been there?"

"No," the ninja admitted. "But my uncle has a few...business associates who may be able to give us some advice if unorthodox sources might prove useful."

"We'll need any help we can get," the Phoenix Force commander said with a nod. "We'll take you to your uncle. After you talk with him, we'll have to get ready to leave for China. I suggest you don't return to your home. The owner of the coffee shop may have recognized you, or the skinheads might describe you to the police. The karate *gi* alone will give them a pretty good idea who you must be since the *dojo* is right across the street from the shop."

"Don't tell me I'm going to get in trouble with the police because I helped beat up some hoodlums," Trent groaned, shaking his head slightly.

"Hell, no," James assured him. "We just have to take off, and there isn't time for answering questions for the cops. We'll have to buy you some clothes and luggage for the trip. Already got a passport and visa ready for you, all made out in the name of Timothy Carson. Get used to the name 'cause you'll be using it while we're in China."

"You fellows think of just about everything," Trent commented. "I can get the necessary tools of *ninjutsu* from Uncle Inoshiro, but I don't know for certain that he'd have spare firearms."

"No problem," Katz assured him. "We have a 12-gauge Remington pump shotgun and a 9 mm Ruger P-85 autoloader for you. I know you favor the .45 Colt pistol, but 9 mm parabellum will be a better choice caliber for this mission. Trying to get .45 ammo in China will be far more difficult."

"I don't like relying on a weapon I'm not familiar with," Trent confessed with a shrug, "but I'll go along with your decision."

"Then let's take you to your uncle and get on with our mission," Katz declared.

"That figures," James muttered, turning the steering wheel. "I finally found a parking space and now we gotta leave."

THE U.S. NAVY aircraft carrier was in port off the coast of Hong Kong in the South China Sea. A Bell UH-1D helicopter rose from the massive decks of the enormous vessel and headed north, across Hong Kong and directly into the Guangdong Province of the People's Republic of China. The American chopper received permission to enter

Chinese territory and continued on to a small airfield near the city of Haifeng.

Phoenix Force and John Trent peered out the cabin windows of the helicopter to get their first look at the People's Republic. The ports were active with a variety of modern vessels and traditional Asian craft, fishing boats and exotic Chinese junks with great elegant sails. Farmers labored in rice paddies inland. Figures clad in cotton "pajamas" and conical hats were busy in the fields of the rich wet soil. Water buffalo pulled carts and plows for the farmers. It was a scene which had been part of life in China for thousands of years.

Haifeng was a small city by Chinese standards. Few modern buildings stood among the crowded collections of simple adobe and bamboo dwellings, yet Haifeng appeared to be changing. Even from a distance, the skeletal frames of new buildings under construction were visible to the bird's-eye view of the men in the chopper. Telephone lines extended across the city, and a few television antennae jutted among the rooftops.

A network of roads radiated from Haifeng. Buses, bikers and a few automobiles shared the roads with carts drawn by buffalo and yak, as well as a few hauled by human beasts of burden. The busiest roads were those leading to the Guangdong capital of Canton. The Bell copter was only authorized to travel to the airfield near Haifeng. The UH-1D was a relatively short-range craft anyway, and flying to Canton would require more fuel than the chopper could handle.

It approached the airfield. An aged Russian-made twin-engine airplane stood on a runway. Three weather-worn hangars and a tower were the only structures at the field. Two large black cars were parked near the hangars, and several figures stood by the vehicles and watched the copter hover above the field.

The UH-1D descended to a landing pad. It touched down and a cloud of dust rose from the current of the rotor blades. Phoenix Force opened the sliding door and began to file out of the craft. Four of the men by the cars walked forward. Two were attired in business suits with plain white shirts, dark neckties and straw fedora-style hats. The other two wore military uniforms, white gloves, and caps with polished bills. Other uniformed men stood by the cars. They carried Type 56 assault rifles.

"Have we arrived in time?" Katz called out to the men who approached, using the prearranged password.

"We know who you are," a short Chinese in a suit replied in fluent English with a clipped BBC British accent. His face was round, but his torso was slight, and he appeared to be slightly bowlegged. Dark glasses concealed his eyes, although the morning sun was still soft in the cloud-laced sky. "Please, place your luggage on the ground and step away from it."

"This doesn't sound friendly," Rafael Encizo remarked as he lowered two aluminum suitcases to the ground.

"Do as you are told," a slender, stern-faced Chinese officer snapped, a gloved hand resting on the button-flap holster on his hip.

"I don't think they intend to be friendly," John Trent added as he stepped away from his luggage and left his hands in plain view of the Chinese welcome wagon.

"Would you fellows mind giving us an explanation for this?" Calvin James asked, holding his hands at shoulder level. He did not like the look on the face of the officer who seemed ready to draw his piece at any moment. "Thought you fellas were told we came to *work* with you."

"That may have changed," the Chinese who seemed to be in command declared. "You will please come with us, and we shall discuss this matter in private."

"A man from the American embassy was supposed to meet us as well," Gary Manning stated, "a Mr. Ross?"

"Oh, yes," the leader of the reception committee said with a slight smile. "Mr. Ross is CIA. His real name is Baskins. He was formerly a case officer in Taiwan where he was known as Barrett and claimed to be a reporter for UPI. 'Mr. Ross' wore a toupee in Taiwan, but now he's had a hair transplant. Not terribly successful, I'm afraid. He also wears contact lenses now. That's about all I recall from the files on the man in our office in Beijing. There was something concerning the man's fondness of Eurasian girls, but I shall be discreet."

"The Social Affairs Department is very efficient," Katz said with a nod. "Are you Mr. Pao?"

"That's the name I'm using at this time," the leader confessed and nodded in reply. "You must be Mr. Gray. You've used that name before. We have a rather thin record on you, too. Little more than a physical description and a vague account of a matter, which occurred in Hong Kong two years ago. It is rare that SAD fails to learn many details about anyone who operates in this part of the world for very long. You must not have spent much time in the Orient."

"Long enough to appreciate the good manners, which generally accompany dealings with the Chinese people," David McCarter stated. The Briton's usually sharp tongue was blunted as he knew rudeness among Asians is regarded to be only slightly less acceptable behavior than child molesting.

"Terrorism is a worse form of bad manners," Pao replied. "That is what we must talk about. Please, do not delay. Major Hsing is impatient and a bit worried about your helicopter. He believes there may be missiles and machine guns on board. No doubt you have noticed his men are well armed. If there is the slightest reason to suspect something is wrong, they have orders to fire.''

"That could sure hurt Sino-American relations,'' James commented.

"We have no wish to do that," Pao insisted, "but there is a matter of face involved."

"Well, I'm confused," Manning admitted. "What the hell happened? We just got here. What do you think we did, spit out the window of the helicopter?"

"The best thing for us to do is go with these gentlemen and hope we get some answers that make sense," Katz declared.

"Very wise," Pao said. "We will, of course, have to frisk you for weapons. The major's men will bring your luggage and fuel up the helicopter so it may have a safe journey back to the aircraft carrier it came from."

"Very well, Mr. Pao," Katz agreed. They did not seem to have much choice under the circumstances.

"We may have really stepped in it this time," Encizo whispered, his voice barely loud enough for Katz to hear.

"We'll just have to find out," the Israeli replied.

"I just hope we don't find out that this whole mission was a setup," the Cuban muttered grimly, "and that we walked right into a trap."

6

Phoenix Force and John Trent were loaded inside the long black automobiles. The cars were similar to Russian ZIL limousines. There was ample room inside the vehicles for the six visitors, four soldiers, Pao and another SAD agent named Yang. Major Hsing and more of his troops accompanied the limos in Land Rovers driven from the hangars. The military vehicles escorted the cars as the caravan drove onto the road to Canton.

James glanced out the rear window and saw the Bell chopper rise from the field. The pilot and crew would head back to the carrier and James wondered if the rest of them would ever leave China alive. The black warrior sat in the back of a limo with Katz and Manning. Mr. Pao and a tough-looking army sergeant sat opposite the Phoenix commandos. The NCO had a Type 51 pistol in a shoulder holster. Calvin James recognized the pistol. He had seen such "Chinese Tokarevs" in Vietnam. A few NVA and Vietcong had carried the same make pistols. Red China had once been a supporter of North Vietnam during Mao's rule.

Odd how the world changed, James thought. Red China and the Soviet Union had been "the other side" as long as James could remember. They were viewed as Communist superpowers that were trying to devour the rest of the world. They were the real forces he thought he had gone to Vietnam to fight. Communist expansion had been the primary concern of American foreign policies since World

War II. Yet Mainland China had supposedly changed dramatically since the death of Chairman Mao. Even Russia was allegedly going through the process of *glasnost*—"openness."

Maybe, the black commando mused. It sure didn't seem like the People's Republic had become a cheerful, cooperative ally when the SAD and armed troops had been waiting for Phoenix Force to arrive and whisked them swiftly away in a government convoy, virtually at gunpoint.

"All right, Mr. Pao," Katz began, resting his prosthesis across his lap. "Can you explain this to us now?"

"I believe so," Pao answered. "The soldiers know the basics concerning this mission. Perhaps you don't know what happened a few hours ago. The news may not have reached the international press just yet."

"What news is that?" Manning inquired.

"Seventeen Chinese civilians were killed, and several others were seriously injured by a terrorist attack in Shanghai," the SAD agent declared. "An explosion occurred in a busy marketplace. Witnesses also saw several gunmen who opened fire on the crowd with automatic rifles. Several survivors with military background identified the weapons as American-made M-16 assault rifles. Indeed, slugs examined by ballistic personnel have confirmed that the bullets were 5.56 mm, the same caliber, which is used for the M-16. Cartridge casings were also found at the positions of the gunmen. The printing on the cartridges was in romanized letters and numbers, not Chinese."

The SAD agent paused and removed his dark glasses. His dark eyes observed the three foreigners with an unblinking gaze as he continued. "The witnesses also described the gunmen as Caucasians, and they appeared to be Americans or Europeans."

"And you think this may be linked to our mission here in China?" Katz said with a sigh. "That would really be rather foolish for us to come casually strolling into your country like sheep to the slaughter if we were involved."

"Naturally you would tell us if you were part of a CIA plot against the People's Republic?" Pao asked with a slight smile.

"Probably not," the Israeli admitted, "but I'm certainly not going to confess to something we're not involved in, either. Come now, Mr. Pao. Do you honestly believe this?"

"I most sincerely believe in the national security of the People's Republic of China and the necessity to protect it," the SAD man replied.

"I understand that," Katz assured him. "However, your interests and the interests of your country are the same as our own in this matter. You know why we're here. More than two dozen tourists from America and Europe have been victims of terrorism in China. Terrorism carried out by Chinese."

"That is not a proven fact, Mr. Gray," Pao stated. "The terrorists who attacked the tourists have not been identified. They wore disguises and masks. It is possible they are not Chinese or even Asian."

"You don't think the CIA murdered tourists and then turned around and decided to kill a bunch of Chinese as well?" Gary Manning inquired. "That doesn't make much sense, Mr. Pao. What the hell would the Company have to gain by such a tactic? America and China are on better terms than they have been since World War II. Why would CIA want to screw that up?"

"I have no idea," Pao admitted. "Personally I'm not convinced the Americans are responsible."

"Glad to hear that," James announced. "This whole business sounds like a setup, man. White dudes with

American-made weapons are considerate enough to attack Chinese civilians and leave a ton of evidence to point at CIA and Uncle Sam? The Company has done some dumb stuff in the past, but they'd have to be brain-damaged to pull a stunt like that."

"Do you have another theory?' Pao asked.

"We don't have any information," James answered, rolling his eyes toward the ceiling of the car. "We just got here. If we don't know any details, we can't come up with any intelligent suggestions. We could guess the Martians did it with all the facts we've learned so far."

"Which acts of terrorism are you talking about, Mr...?"

"Call me Johnson," James replied. "And I was talking about the attacks on Western tourists *and* the slaughter in Shanghai. God, that sounds like a movie title, doesn't it?"

"Perhaps it is," Pao remarked, a twinkle of amusement in his eyes. "One of those dreadful kung fu movies they make in Hong Kong. So you believe the same people who committed the murderous assaults on the tourists also attacked our civilians?"

"We've seen terrorists use such tactics before," Katz stated. "It's a very old trick. The enemy gets your side and our side to fight. Each mistakenly believes the other to be responsible. The real enemy simply waits for us to destroy each other."

"An interesting theory, considering you don't have any facts." Pao smiled consideringly. "You may be right. China and United States certainly have one common enemy who would certainly be capable of such a bold and complex scheme. Of course I refer to the Soviet Union and their KGB spy organization."

"It's possible," Katz agreed, "but we can't prove anything or do anything to stop the terrorists without the cooperation of the SAD and CIA. If you aren't going to oblige us, we may as well arrange to go back to the aircraft carrier and let you handle this mess on your own. Bear in mind, China's efforts to establish good relations with the United States and the other Western nations will be hurt if the terrorism continues."

"I am aware of that," Pao said with a slight nod. He leaned back and placed the tips of his fingers together in a tentlike manner at his lips. He regarded the three Phoenix commandos thoughtfully. "Well, gentlemen. We'll have to try to arrange some way to send you back or work together."

The convoy reached Canton. An ancient city, its origins dating back to before the third century B.C., Canton had been a center of culture, trade and agriculture since the Ming Dynasty...if not earlier. Persian and Indian traders were doing business in Canton before the Portuguese came to China in the fifteenth century.

Modern Canton was still an important Chinese city and more successful than ever. The capital of Guangdong Province had a population of more than three million. Great apartment complexes and office buildings towered above the busy streets. As the vehicles crossed Haichu Bridge, the passengers saw the factories along the Pearl River and numerous vessels moving through the waters. Canton had become a major site for Chinese industry, with automobiles and machinery as important products. Chemicals, fertilizers and food were also processed in the city.

Monuments to the past stood among the structures of the present. Sha Mian island was visible in the distance. It was little more than a sandbank in the river, yet it had once been a site for unrestricted trade with the West and European settlements. The convoy moved into the flow of traffic within the heart of the city. Pao switched on the two-radio unit and spoke into the mouthpiece in rapid Chinese. A voice replied in the same language. None of the three Phoenix Force pros understood Mandarin, but they noticed the Land Rovers pulled away from the limos. Pao must have ordered Major Hsing and his men to separate from the convoy to avoid drawing more attention as the cars approached their destination.

However, there was no doubt the thousands of people on the street realized the limos were government cars. The majority of traffic consisted of trucks, buses and bicycle riders. Private ownership of automobiles was still rare in China. The few cars that traveled the streets of Canton were small economy models and taxi cabs. The big black autos stood out like a pair of ravens at a swan convention.

The ornate rooftop of the pagoda of the Temple of Six Banyan trees stood above a column of shops and small restaurants, visible to the passengers as the limos passed by. Other vehicles made room for the government cars. Unlike many cities in the West, drivers and bike riders seemed polite and considerate, regardless of the amount of traffic. The crowds were enormous, but everyone seemed busy. People moved to and fro as if eager to reach their destination.

The limos pulled into the garage of an office building, then proceeded to park in twin spaces beside three other large black automobiles. Pao told the visitors to get out of the car. Katz, James and Manning emerged from the limo. David McCarter, Rafael Encizo and John Trent climbed out of the other car, accompanied by Agent Yang and an armed Chinese NCO.

"Did you blokes enjoy the tour as much as we did?" McCarter asked sarcastically.

"Oh, yeah," James answered. "Got some great flashing glimpses of all kinds of neat stuff."

"We don't get to visit many of the historic landmarks when we travel," Manning added, "but we generally get to see things tourists don't. Like terrorist strongholds, covert battlefields in the middle of the night, gangsters in sleazy dives. Who could ask for more?"

"Please, follow me," Pao instructed, still polite, but firm. His request was clearly a thinly disguised command.

"Excuse me, Mr. Pao," Encizo began. "Major Hsing has our gear, including our personal side arms and our bladed weapons."

The Cuban was very uncomfortable without his usual array of personal weaponry. Encizo generally carried a Heckler & Koch P-9S 9 mm pistol, a Walther PPK, a Cold Steel Tanto and a Gerber Mark I fighting dagger. That lineup did not even include the H&K MP-5 submachine gun he favored for serious combat situations.

"Bloody right," McCarter added. The Briton also felt naked without his trusty Browning Hi-Power in shoulder leather under his arm. The pistol was as much a part of McCarter as his rib cage. "Just when do we get our weapons back?"

"This is the People's Republic of China," Pao answered. "Not the Wild West or Northern Ireland."

"We were told Beijing authorized us to carry concealed weapons," Katz told him. "In fact you took our firearm permits when you confiscated our passports and visas. If you'll examine them, you'll notice they have been signed by the Minister of National Security of your country and the President of the United States."

"Very impressive documents," Pao confirmed. "I know they are genuine because the minister made an emergency trip to the United States after the attacks on the Western tourists. I was, of course, told about this agreement between Beijing and Washington. However, recent events change that. You will not be authorized to carry any weapons until the Social Affairs Department and the Central Committee decide otherwise."

"Jesus," Calvin James muttered. "We might as well head home if you guys are gonna insist on these restrictions. If we catch up with the terrorists, what are we supposed to do? Throw salt on their tails? Tell them to throw down their arms and surrender in the name of the law, or we'll make them stay after class and clean erasers?"

"Why don't you worry about those matters when we locate the terrorists?" Pao suggested.

"You've never gone up against terrorists, have you?" Encizo inquired. It was not a true question because the Cuban already knew the answer. "They're different than soldiers, gangsters or even espionage agents. They're far more ruthless and more apt to use violence without provocation. If we even get close, they'll attack. We'd damn well better be ready for them when that happens."

"You're in no position to make demands," Agent Yang declared, his voice hard. Yang's English was not as fluent as Pao's, and it had a singsong quality. Chinese words vary in tone inflections. This language trait had been carried over to Yang's English.

"We'll discuss this upstairs," Pao insisted as he led the group to an elevator at the end of the underground garage.

They filed into the elevator car. It was a freight lift, large enough to carry truckloads of cargo. There was ample room for two dozen passengers in the elevator, but Pao dismissed the watchdogs. Only the two SAD agents, Phoenix Force and John Trent rode the lift to the eighth floor. The car arrived at an immaculate corridor, almost hospital-sterile in appearance.

Pao and Yang escorted the visitors past several doors to a room at the end of the hall. Pao knocked and spoke a short, curt sentence in Chinese. The door opened, and a large Asian appeared at the doorway. He bowed and stepped aside to allow the men to enter.

It was a conference room with a long table, several chairs and a small cabinet with a teapot and numerous small china cups on top of the counter. A water cooler stood in one corner, and a flag with the red banner and yellow star of the People's Republic stood in an opposite corner.

A middle-aged Caucasian male sat alone at the conference table. He did not look happy. In fact he appeared to be on the verge of a nervous breakdown. The fellow was dressed in a wrinkled suit, striped tie and a white Arrow shirt with a sweat-stained collar. His skull was mostly exposed, with a few short spikelike hairs jutting out among the trio of long sparse strands he had combed over his dome. Katz recalled what Pao had said about the hair transplant Mr. Ross had recently acquired. The Israeli agreed with Pao's opinion. The transplant had certainly been less than successful.

"Mr. Ross—" Pao began, and indicated Phoenix Force with a gesture "—these are the gentlemen we've been expecting. Please, forgive me if I don't introduce them. I don't know all of the names they are using, and everyone in this room is going by a cover name anyway. It seems a bit pointless, don't you think?"

"Listen, Pao," Ross began in an angry tone. "I demand to talk to my embassy. That's the United States embassy in Beijing."

"And I shall grant that request in time," Pao replied. He turned to Phoenix Force. "Please be seated and we shall continue our conversation."

"Do we have to?" McCarter asked with an annoyed sigh. The Briton dumped his rump in a chair and reached for the pack of Player's cigarettes in his jacket pocket before he remembered that the pack and lighter had been confiscated.

"Cigarette?" Pao asked, taking a pack from his jacket. "I got these in Hong Kong."

He handed the pack to McCarter. The Briton raised his eyebrows with surprise. They were Player's cigarettes. "I admire your taste," he commented, taking one from the pack.

"From your accent I thought you might favor British brands," Pao said with a smile, offering a lighter to McCarter. "In truth, so do I. I'm afraid Chinese tobacco isn't much to brag about. Fortunately Hong Kong is still a British dependency and cigarettes are among the imports. I'm not sure what will happen in 1997 when ownership of Hong Kong reverts back to China. I hope we'll continue to import British cigarettes."

"How quaint," Ross muttered. "Have you guys gotten any further with Pao than I have? He seems to think this mess is a CIA plot."

"Mr. Pao is just being careful, Mr. Ross," Katz replied, gesturing for McCarter to pass him the cigarettes. "I doubt that he really believes the Company is responsible, but he has to consider every possibility."

"You understand perfectly," Pao said with a nod. "In fact I have my own theory about who the terrorists might be. We spoke briefly in the car about the possibility the Soviet KGB could be responsible. I consider the Russians to be the most likely suspects."

Katz stuck a Player's into his mouth. He would have preferred a Camel or Turkish Specials, but the popular British brand would serve to satisfy his nicotine craving. The Israeli considered, for perhaps the fifty thousandth time, that he ought to quit smoking. He was approaching... well, he considered he was really at the peak of middle age. Although he was still healthy, stronger and faster than most men half his age, Katz realized the years took their toll. His endurance was not as great as it had once been, and his body took longer to recover from injuries and bruises. Smoking would only reduce his wind, help the aging process eat away at his body.

But Katz lit the cigarette anyway.

"We've encountered a number of terrorist operations, which were run by the KGB," the Israeli declared. "The Soviet Committee for State Security is certainly capable of such actions. However, the Soviets have a great deal of domestic problems right now, and quite a few abroad as well. Especially where the Soviets have set up puppet governments with occupying forces in those countries."

"You mean Afghanistan?" Ross asked. "I thought they were pulling troops out of there."

"The current government is still one the Soviets put in power back in 1978 and everyone knows it," Katz replied. "Besides, the Soviets also have their hands full with Vietnam, Angola and Mozambique in Africa, activities in Central America and, of course, Eastern Europe."

"The Russians have spread themselves a bit too thin and they're finding out it's damn hard to hang on to so many territories, even when they're operating indirectly through puppet powers," Encizo added. The Cuban had formerly been a freedom fighter against Castro's regime, and he knew the Soviet Union was the true power behind Fidel. Encizo had a personal reason to keep abreast of Soviet policies. "That's what this *glasnost* business is all about, in my opinion. It's not that the Kremlin has become good guys overnight. They just realized they bit off more than they could chew."

"This little chitchat about Soviet politics would be just fine," McCarter said impatiently, "if it was getting us any closer to finding the bloody terrorists."

"Masters has a point," Gary Manning stated, using McCarter's cover name. "We should be looking at the evidence and seeing which direction it points, instead of talking about who *might* be responsible."

"I say the evidence points at the Hui," Yang announced. The inflection of his words made the sentence sound like a cross between an angry command and a puzzled question.

"Who?" Encizo asked.

"The Hui are Chinese Muslims," John Trent explained. He had barely said a word since arriving in China, and the others had almost forgotten he was in the room. "A definite minority group in the People's Republic. I believe most of the Hui are located in provinces to the northwest. Correct?"

"Yes," Pao said, surprised by Trent's knowledge. "The Hui Autonomous Region is in Ningsia. They are also located in Gansu and Qinghai Provinces. I doubt if their combined population is more than six and half, perhaps seven million, total."

"Six and a half million is still a hell of a lot of people," Manning declared.

"Not in China," Pao corrected.

"Mr. Yang," Katz began, turning to face the lesser-ranking SAD agent. "Why do you suspect that the Chinese Muslims are involved in terrorism?"

"Surely you have heard of the Islamic Jihad?" Yang answered. "Muslim fanatics are carrying out acts of senseless violence throughout the world. The Middle East, Persian Gulf, Europe, everywhere. The followers of Mohammed even kidnapped Soviet officials in Lebanon, and many times they have hijacked planes to take American hostages."

"Hold on a second," James began. "There are Muslims involved in terrorism, no argument on that, but the majority of Muslims *aren't* terrorists and don't approve of their tactics. Has there ever been any proof that the Hui have been connected with the Ayatollah's Shiite extremist movement or Black September or maybe a radical branch of the PLO?''

"Nothing solid," Pao answered. "Rumors and accusations, but no real proof."

"When you find your rice has been eaten and rat droppings by the spot," Yang declared as if quoting great wisdom, "you do not need to see the rodent to know who is responsible."

"So where's this rat shit, pal?" McCarter asked.

"Ningsia," Yang answered. "And that is where we will find the terrorists."

"Well," Ross said with a sigh, "at least it's a place to start."

"Sounds more like a waste of time to me," Manning replied, shaking his head. "I think we should check out Shanghai, where the last terrorist attack occurred, and the other sites of the attacks on tourists."

"I think we should get our goddamn guns back," McCarter said with a slight pout.

"Not yet," Pao replied. "However, Major Hsing will bring your belongings, including your weapons, to Beijing. That's where we'll have our base of operations. SAD headquarters and the American embassy are there. Also, special sections of the Social Affairs Department and the Central External Liaison Department will be available to us. Computers, satellite communications, specialized equipment and weapons, all will be much easier to acquire if we are in Beijing."

"Would it be possible for me to check some things on my own?" John Trent inquired. "There are a couple possible leads I would like to look into, but I will have to do it alone."

"What sort of leads?" Yang asked with a frown.

"Individuals who would be very uncooperative if the SAD or any police or military accompanied me," Trent explained.

"What sort of individuals?" Yang demanded. His sing-song accent made the question sound as if he was close to hysteria. "Rebels of some sort? Those students who want more democratic reforms? Bah! They would have anarchy in China if they had their way. You will learn nothing useful from those fools."

"I'm sorry, Mr...." Pao cast an inquiring glance at Trent, who in turn looked at Katz.

"Carson," the Phoenix leader said hastily. "Timothy Carson."

"Mr. Carson," Pao continued, "I'm afraid I can't allow you or any of your party to be at large without SAD escort. Although I personally do not believe you gentlemen or the United States of America are involved in the terrorist activities, you are all still technically suspects until events occur to alter these conditions."

"So we're restricted from going anywhere or doing anything without chaperons?" Encizo said with disgust. "And we can't be armed, either."

"Isn't that just bloody dandy," McCarter added bitterly.

7

Yakov Katzenelenbogen summed up his impressions: Ningsia Province had little in common with Canton. It was like stepping into another world, a different world from a different time. Although there were a few modern cities in the Hui Autonomous Region, the majority of the Chinese Muslims lived in villages and farming communities. Most lived in much the same manner as their ancestors had two hundred years earlier.

The Phoenix commander and David McCarter sat in the back seat of the Land Rover. Pao was in the front, next to the driver, an NCO familiar with the Ningsia Region. Major Hsing and three other Chinese soldiers followed in another Rover. The troops were armed with Type 56 assault rifles and Type 50 submachine guns. They seemed suspicious of the two Phoenix Force commandos and watched the pair as if they expected Katz and McCarter to suddenly jump from the lead vehicle and attempt to escape.

Even if the Phoenix pair intended to flee, Ningsia did not offer much to run to. The Land Rovers had passed some forests of broad-leaved trees, not unlike those found throughout most of the United States. But the farther north they headed, the less vegetation appeared. Much of Ningsia was dry and poorly irrigated. Rocks, sand and sparse weeds dominated much of the landscape.

"Hard to believe this is China, isn't it?" McCarter remarked to Katz. "Reminds me of parts of central Oman. Except it's a bit cooler here."

"Yes," Katz agreed, although he would have compared the area with Jordan rather than Oman. "I understand the northwest provinces tend to have a colder climate than the rest of China."

"Cold winds coming in from the north," Pao explained, glancing over his shoulder at the Occidental passengers. "The Soviet Union and the People's Republic of Mongolia are to the north. Their climate is less temperate. We even get Siberian air currents at times. Nothing positive ever comes from those borders. Even Mao learned that the Russians weren't our friends. It took the fat bastard more than two decades to figure it out. Anyone in Chinese intelligence could have told him that long before 1968."

"You haven't been with SAD that long, have you?" Katz inquired. "You don't look older than late thirties or early forties."

"No," Pao confirmed. "I wasn't with intelligence then, but I'm old enough to remember Mao's so-called 'Cultural Revolution' and the 'Great Leap Forward.' Mind you, I'm not saying everything Mao Tse-tung did was wrong. Education improved dramatically. At one time, in fact throughout most of our history, the vast majority of Chinese could not read or write. Now, seventy-five percent of the population is literate. Science, technology, productivity and health care had improved under Mao. Yet none of that changes the fact that Chairman Mao was a modern-day emperor and a tyrant."

"Things must have changed a great deal since Mao's death," McCarter commented.

"I wouldn't dare talk this way if it hadn't," Pao confessed with a slight laugh. "We're still Communists, of course, but we've been going through changes, which I personally approve of. China can't go back to the old isolationist policies of the past. Every time that happened our growth ceased and we started to slide backward. But China survived. Emperors, foreign rulers, dictators all come and go, but China remains."

"I hope you're right," Katz told him. "You speak excellent English, Mr. Pao. Did you learn it here or abroad?"

"I was once an undercover agent in Hong Kong," Pao explained with a shrug. "A 'sleeper' agent. I was stationed in Hong Kong for six years, so I had ample time to perfect my English. That was back in the early seventies. I would have cut your throats if Beijing ordered it."

"And now?" Katz inquired.

"Now I'd order someone else to cut your throats for me," Pao said with a faint smile. "Let's hope it doesn't come to that, eh?"

THE AFTERNOON SUN COMPETED against the chilly winds with little success. The cloud cover blocked some of the sun's rays and cast a disquieting early twilight across the terrain. The cars approached a village near the city of Guyuan. The walls surrounding the village were made of stone and mortar, and the buildings within the wall were simple structures, except for the large white brick mosque at the center of the village. The teardrop shaped dome reflected the traditions of Arab or Persian architecture rather than the graceful curved roofs, elegant eaves and ornate figurines of Chinese pagodas.

"I still feel like I'm back in Oman," McCarter stated, pointing at the fields beyond the village walls.

Katz was surprised to see stalks of wheat swaying in the chilly breeze. Then he recalled that wheat was the second most important crop in Mainland China. Even more surprising were the people laboring in the field. Men dressed in baggy trousers, pleated jackets and turbans cut down the wheat with machetelike blades. Women, bundled in long peasant dresses with cowled headgear complete with face scarfs, gathered up the harvest and loaded it into a cart. And the beast of burden was what surprised Phoenix Force most of all. A camel was harnessed before the cart, a strap between its massive twin humps.

McCarter stared at the camel as a man tugged at the reins to the stubborn beast, clucking his tongue to try to urge the animal to move. Something about the animal was different than the camels he had seen in Oman and the Middle East. The Briton snorted aloud when he realized what it was. It was so obvious. The other camels had been *dromedary* camels with a single hump. The two-humped *Bactrian* was native to China and Mongolia. There was nothing remarkable about Chinese farmers using camels for beasts of burden aside from McCarter's own preconceived notions about what to expect in China.

The Land Rovers approached the entrance of the village walls. There was some commotion in the slate-paved streets. Women and children retreated indoors while the men gathered in a cluster to receive the visitors. They appeared grim, as though expecting trouble, their lips sealed in firm lines.

No one could blame the Hui for distrust of the government. The Chinese Muslims had known more than their share of persecution. When Communist rule first came to China, all religions were officially eliminated. Temples, churches and mosques were taken over by the state. Many were destroyed, others converted to museums or schools for the new faith of Maoism.

Since the majority of Chinese were Taoists, Confucianists or Buddhists, the Muslims and even smaller Christian population were already regarded with a degree of distrust and suspicion. The quasi-secular nature of Confucianism allowed its followers to be less affected than other religions. Also many Chinese tended to regard religion as a personal family-centered matter and put little importance on temples and services, so giving lip service to the demands of the state was not the hardship experienced by many other cultures. Besides, it is not uncommon in the Orient for an individual to claim more than one religion. Fatalism is a national trait among the Chinese. If one could not be a Buddhist publicly, one could still be a Buddhist privately, or simply endorse Taoism or Confucianism if that was more convenient at the time.

That attitude might seem strange, even irreverent to most Westerners, yet it is better understood in the light of China's long history of emperors and foreign rule. Monarchs would occasionally declare one faith or another as the state religion. Since to the Chinese that was politics—a subject the Chinese have generally regarded as far less important than family—they tended to view such decisions as more nonsense from the emperor. Chairman Mao was just a variation of the emperors of the past, so the Chinese regarded his decrees in much the same manner.

There were exceptions, of course. Thousands of Buddhist monks were killed because they protested Mao's ban on religion. The Islamic Hui defied the Communists and stubbornly continued their faith more openly than most. Thus, the Hui were frequently victims of Mao's soldiers and the fanatic violence of the Red Guard.

The new constitution of 1978 granted Chinese citizens the right to practice whatever religion they wished, while still protecting the rights of atheists and those who wished to propagate atheism. Yet the Islamic Hui had suffered too much for too long to trust the government or the military. The arrival of two army Land Rovers, with four soldiers among the passengers, naturally alarmed the village.

Katz looked at the stern, strong faces of the Hui farmers who stood waiting for the vehicles to enter the village. He admired their courage. They were ready to uphold what they believed in, even though they suspected it could be dangerous. In many ways the persecution of the Hui was similar to that of the Jews in Europe during the Nazi reign of terror. He felt empathy for the Hui and understood their apprehension.

"How's your Chinese these days?" Katz whispered to McCarter, as they heard Pao launch into conversation with the Hui spokesman.

"Not too good," the Briton admitted, "but I've been able to follow the conversation so far. Pao is trying to get the Hui to relax, but they're not buying it. He asked how they were doing and the chieftain asked 'why?' Not a great start."

Pao and the Hui spokesman exchanged more words. The conversation was rapid and contained too many words with varied inflection for McCarter's limited Chinese vocabulary. Pao had stepped from the Land Rover, but signaled for the others to stay put. The SAD agent bowed and gestured with open hands to show he meant no harm. The Hui remained stiff, formally polite, but far from relaxed.

Katz did not need a translator to see things were not going well. The Hui obviously wanted nothing to do with the government visitors, and the soldiers made them particularly nervous. Many of the Muslims carried large knives, hoes and axes. Major Hsing and his troops seemed ready to go for their guns at any sign of trouble. The Israeli suddenly stepped from the Land Rover.

"Assa-la-mo Ahla-kum," he announced and bowed deeply.

The Hui was startled. Pao turned and glared at Katz as the farmers spoke among themselves in excited whispers. The soldiers were confused and uncertain of what might happen next.

"What language are you speaking?" Pao demanded. "What did you say?"

"Just a greeting in Arabic," Katz replied.

"Arabic?" Pao was confused and irritated by Katz's action.

"Let him be," McCarter urged. "He knows what he's doing."

The Hui chief stepped forward and bowed toward Katz. *"Assa-la-mo Ahla-kum,"* he told the Israeli. *"Ana isme Quan."*

"I am honored to meet you, Chief Quan," Katz replied in the same language. "My name is Gray. May Allah grant you and your people prosperity and peace."

"This is the first time a white foreigner has spoken to me in Arabic," Quan stated. "How did you know I would understand?"

"As leader of your village, I assumed you would be an Islamic scholar," Katz explained. "The language of the Koran is Arabic. Every good Muslim knows the Koran, and a scholar would read it in the language of Mohammed."

"You flatter me, Mr. Gray," Quan replied. "Yet compliments cost the giver nothing, and only a fool values them too highly."

"A man considers another to be a fool at great peril," Katz stated. "Since I know you to be a scholar, I would certainly not mistake you for a fool, Chief Quan. We come in peace to ask you questions concerning troubles, which plague China and threaten the welfare of my fellow countrymen as well."

"What country would that be?" Quan asked.

"Are we not all children of Allah?"

"You speak well," the Hui chief said with a nod. "Ask your questions, Mr. Gray. First, however, I must ask one of you. Why are those soldiers with you?"

"The Beijing command insisted on an armed escort," Katz replied. "There has been much violence. Senseless violence against innocent persons. Chinese and visitors from the West."

"There has been no violence among my people," Quan stated. "And none committed by them. Beijing suspects the Hui are responsible? That is why you are here?"

"Some suspect it," Katz answered with a sigh. "You've heard of the Ayatollah's jihad?"

"Ayatollah?" Quan frowned. "We are Sunni Muslims. Why should we care if a Shiite leader chooses to declare a holy war?"

"I understand," the Phoenix Force commander said. "Have you heard anything about terrorist activity? Perhaps rumors of secret camps where armed groups have gathered? Training camps where soldiers have not fired automatic weapons in the past?"

"La," Quan replied. "No. I know nothing about such things. I will ask my people if they have heard anything about such matters."

"That will be appreciated," Katz assured him.

The chief turned toward the villagers. His body suddenly jerked backward as a bullet punched through his torso. Katz saw the blood spurt from the exit wound under Quan's left shoulder blade. The explosion of the assassin's weapon came a split second later. The farmers cried out in horror and outrage as they saw their leader collapse onto the ground before them, a bullet hole in his chest.

"He's at the wall!" David McCarter shouted as he jumped from the Land Rover.

The Briton had glimpsed the muzzle-flash of the sniper's rifle when the shot was fired. He saw little else except the top of the killer's head with a Chinese army cap canted back on the gunman's skull. McCarter immediately bailed out of the vehicle and hit the ground in a fast shoulder roll.

He tumbled beside an adobe dwelling for cover. The Phoenix pro instinctively reached inside his jacket for the Browning Hi-Power, but the pistol was not in shoulder leather under his arm.

"Bloody hell," the Briton rasped through clenched teeth.

Hell had indeed erupted in the small Hui community. The sniper snapped the assault rifle's selector switch from semiauto to full-auto and opened fire. Another gunman triggered a second automatic weapon from a position at the top of the wall, about ten yards left of his partner. A vicious hailstorm of high-velocity bullets ripped through the village. Three more Hui farmers fell next to Quan's still form while others dashed for cover.

Yakov Katzenelenbogen had also reacted to the unexpected attack before he realized his reflexes had sent him hurtling for shelter behind a grain silo. Pao followed the Israeli's example and dived behind the silo next to the Phoenix commander. The SAD awkwardly reached inside his coat and dragged a Type 51 pistol from a shoulder holster.

"I'd say we can dismiss the Hui as suspects," Katz commented. The steel hooks of his prosthesis clicked impatiently in helpless frustration. "You wouldn't happened to have a spare weapon? Back-up pistol?"

"Sorry," Pao replied tensely as he worked the slide to his T-51 to chamber the first round. "This is all I have, and I don't think it will do much good at this range."

Suddenly two furious Hui farmers charged around the silo. A screaming Muslim swung a hoe at Pao's head while the other man raised a machete overhead and attacked Katz. Pao held his fire, aware that the Hui believed the snipers were members of his group. The SAD agent did not want to kill any of the farmers because they had mistakenly believed the visitors had set them up to be slaughtered, but the man with the hoe did not share Pao's concern about the agent's welfare.

Pao ducked in time to avoid a skull-cracking blow from the farmer's hoe. The vicious swipe missed the agent's head by scant millimeters and smashed into the stone wall of the silo. Pao's free hand quickly grabbed the shaft of the hoe before the Hui farmer could attempt another attack. The SAD man rammed the muzzle of his pistol under the Muslim's ribs to knock the wind out of his opponent. Pao followed with a hard knee-kick to the gut. The Hui peasant doubled up from the blow, and Pao smacked him behind the ear with the frame of his T-51. The farmer dropped senseless at Pao's feet.

Katz stepped forward and thrust his left arm high. The heel of his palm jammed into the bottom of the other Hui's fist to prevent him from swinging the machete. The Phoenix commander locked his elbow and braced his right foot to form a firm bar with his entire body. The farmer's arm froze overhead, and he was unable to use the big knife in his fist.

The Israeli punched the curved steel of his hooks into his opponent's stomach. Like Pao, Katz did not want to injure or kill the farmer. He grabbed the Muslim's wrist with his single left hand, pulled down forcibly and swung his right arm up to meet the guy's forearm. The farmer's limb slammed across the sturdy steel prosthesis, making his fingers open and the machete fell with a clatter.

Katz held on to the man's wrist with his left hand and rammed his right elbow into the farmer's battered stomach. The Hui groaned and started to fold from the blow. Katz swiftly raised his opponent's arm and jammed his right shoulder under the Muslim's armpit. He bent from the waist and straightened his legs as he pulled on the captive limb. The farmer hurtled over Katz's shoulder and crashed to the ground. Stunned and winded, he would not be getting up for a while, but just in case, Katz kicked the man's machete out of reach to dispose of temptation.

The rattle of automatic fire erupted once more. Two more Hui villagers tumbled to the ground, their torsos ripped open by 7.62 mm slugs. The shots came from the entrance to the walls. Katz turned and saw one of Major Hsing's soldiers fire his Type 56 rifle at the Hui who had failed to reach cover. Stupid bastard! Katz thought angrily. The man must have started shooting into the crowd as a reflex when the first shots were fired.

Hsing shouted at the soldier. The major seemed as alarmed and horrified by his man's actions as Katz was. But the soldier ignored him and continued to spray the village with bullets. Hsing swung the barrel of his own T-56 under the trooper's weapon and pushed it toward the sky. The soldier fired a few harmless rounds into the clouds before Hsing delivered a butt-stroke to the man's left forearm and sent the rifle flying from his grasp.

The aggressors at the wall continued to blast away at the village. Bullets sparked against buildings and houses. Glass shattered from windows. The panicked shouts of men and women filled the air. A wounded farmer tried to crawl for safety, dragging his bullet-shattered leg. A sniper spotted him and nailed the villager with a trio of 7.62 mm slugs.

Pao leaned around the silo and fired two pistol shots at the assassins, but they were more than seventy-five yards away and the T-51 autoloader was a short-range handgun. Pao cursed under his breath when he saw stone chip from a wall where his bullets hit, far from the intended target.

Major Hsing fired his T-56 rifle as he ran to the archway at the mouth of the wall. Bullets struck the top of the wall and forced the enemy gunmen to duck. The major pressed his back to the wall and glanced at McCarter. The British ace had gathered up some fist-sized rocks. He had been unable to find any other sort of weapon. Hsing pulled open the button-flap holster on his hip.

"Masters!" the major called out as he drew his T-51 side arm.

McCarter saw Hsing hold the pistol by the barrel and toss it in an underhand throw to McCarter. The Briton stepped forward and caught the T-51 midair. His fingers instantly responded to the familiar feel of a pistol in his hands. McCarter jacked the slide to chamber a round and moved to the rear of the house he was using for shelter.

Hsing and his troops fired at the gunmen at the wall, although the enemy had avoided shooting at the troops. Katz saw why the snipers did not fire at Hsing's men. The killers were dressed in Chinese army uniforms. The attack was supposed to look like genocide carried out by the military against the Hui. That meant it was a hit-and-run strike. The assassins would pull out within seconds and flee the area, leaving Pao's group to try to convince the farmers they weren't responsible. That seemed pretty unlikely unless they could stop the gunmen from escaping.

"Pao!" Katz shouted in an attempt to be heard above the roar of automatic fire. "Order Hsing's troops to advance on the enemy from *outside* the walls! Circle around the village! Cut off the enemies' escape route! Fast! They'll bolt any second!"

Pao did not question Katz's reasons. His shouted orders were followed by barked commands from Hsing, who also gestured for two men to go right and the others to go left. The panicked soldier could barely move his numb left arm. He gathered up his rifle with one hand while another trooper headed around the perimeter of the wall. The third soldier ducked behind a Land Rover for cover and was reluctant to move, but slowly stood and reached inside the vehicle for his Type 50 subgun.

At least two sniper rounds suddenly crashed into the man's chest and upper arm. He cried out and collapsed next to the vehicle. The soldier cradled the T-50 in his good arm against his chest and huddled low as more bullets punched a trio of holes through the windshield of the Rover. The poor fellow was scared to move and already badly wounded.

Hsing slid a fresh magazine into his T-56 and fired at the enemy position as he broke cover and rushed to his wounded man. Bullets tore up dust geysers near the officer's feet, but Hsing did not seem to notice. Rounds punched into the Land Rover, smashing the latch to the hood and making it pop open like the lid of a jack-in-the-box. Water spilled from the ruptured radiator, and a cloud of hot steam sizzled from the damaged vehicle.

Pao fired a few more ineffective pistol shots at the enemy to help cover Hsing's effort to rescue the soldier. The major seized the wounded man by the collar of his jacket with one hand and held the assault rifle in the other. Hsing awkwardly dragged the soldier to the comparative safety at the stone archway, occasionally firing his T-56 one-handedly at the enemy. Bullets hissed angry trails in the air near the officer, yet Hsing kept moving and reached cover with his injured trooper in tow. The man still clutched the unfired T-50 submachine gun to his chest as if clinging to some sort of magic amulet.

"The major is a brave man," Katz remarked, somewhat surprised, since Hsing had not made a good impression with Phoenix Force when they first met.

"Very brave," Pao agreed, carefully peering around the side of the silo. "I wish he also had X-ray binoculars for eyes so he could locate those damn snipers. I can't see enough of the bastards to get a decent shot at them. Not that I'm the greatest pistol marksman in the world."

"One of the best pistol marksman in the world is trying to get into position to take the enemy out," Katz commented. "The rest of us can keep the gunmen busy so he has a chance to do it."

Hsing called out to them, then tossed the T-50 subgun from the archway to Katz and Pao's position.

The Israeli grabbed the weapon. A stray sniper round tore another clump of earth from the ground inches from the Phoenix commander's fingers. Katz held on to the subgun and hastily rolled back to cover behind the silo with Pao. He examined the T-50. It was a Chinese version of the Soviet PPSh-41, which was similar in design to the old Nazi Schmeisser MP-40 and the French MAT-49. The T-50 weighed about nine pounds, and the magazine contained 35 rounds of 7.62 mm ammo.

"Sure you can handle that thing?" Pao inquired. "I mean, with only one arm..."

"I can manage," Katz assured him as he pulled back the wire stock to the T-50 and locked it into place. "Now, let's see if we can't change the way this battle has been going.

DAVID MCCARTER SPRINTED between the rear of the houses and the east wall of the village. He wished he had his Browning Hi-Power instead of the Type 51 pistol, but it was better than throwing rocks at opponents. The exchange of automatic fire told him that his allies were trying to keep the enemy busy. McCarter also realized the urgency of the situation and that time was something they had precious little of. He hurried along the narrow passage and headed toward the center of the village.

Suddenly an angry young Hui farmer appeared from the side of a dwelling and launched himself at McCarter, screaming in rage.

The Briton held his fire. The farmer was unarmed and, understandably, mistook McCarter for an enemy. The

Phoenix ace slipped his index finger from the trigger and gripped the T-51 by the frame with the butt jutting from the bottom of his fist. The farmer charged, his hands going for McCarter's throat, his face wild with fury.

McCarter raised his arms and slammed the forearms against the inner wrists of the farmer's grasping limbs. The twin blows knocked the Hui's arms wide apart, and the hands were wrenched from the Briton's neck. McCarter's left fist hooked a punch to the side of his opponent's jaw, followed by an uppercut with the right. The butt of the pistol clipped the farmer hard under the chin. The young man staggered backward from the blow, blood oozing from his lips, but still on his feet.

"Tough bloke," McCarter rasped and snap-kicked the farmer in the abdomen.

The Hui doubled up with a painful gasp. McCarter hit him in the side of the skull with another left hook and finally put him out of commission for a while. The British commando continued to move toward the heart of the village until he reached a house directly across from the mosque.

The mosque was small, only two stories high, not including the large graceful dome. It was simple in design and construction, yet well cared for by the devout Muslims of the village. The white brick walls were clean and showed little wear from exposure to all sorts of weather. A minaret, as tall as the mosque itself, stood alongside the Islamic house of worship. The tower was traditionally used by the muezzin to call the faithful to prayer.

The snipers still seemed preoccupied with the shots fired by Hsing and Pao. McCarter moved to the edge of the house and judged the distance to the mosque. Ten yards, he figured. Not far, but far enough to present a target for the enemy. McCarter took a deep breath. The gunmen would not continue to battle with the soldiers much longer, although the gunfire beyond the walls suggested Hsing's men had cut off the enemy's avenue of escape.

The Briton broke cover and dashed for the mosque. A burst of automatic fire snarled from the wall. McCarter dived forward, tucked in his head and landed on a shoulder. The British ace rolled to the base of the minaret. Bullets whined against the stone tower as the Phoenix commando crouched in its shelter.

He entered the door at the foot of the minaret and quickly mounted the ladder within the tower. McCarter climbed to the muezzin platform at the top and waited behind the supports of the roof. He spotted a sniper along the wall, head and shoulders barely exposed. There appeared to be a sort of catwalk at the top of the wall. The snipers used the stone rim at the summit of the wall for cover and poked their weapons over the top to fire at the Hui and the soldiers.

The target offered by the gunman was small, but it was less than ten feet from the top of the minaret. McCarter could have clipped off the guy's earlobes at that distance with his Browning, but accurate shooting with a strange and unfamiliar weapon was another matter. The T-51 was also a smaller caliber than the 9 mm Hi-Power McCarter favored. That meant the 7.65 mm rounds from the T-51 would have less take-down force.

McCarter held the "Chinese Tokarev" in both hands, raised the gun and aimed as quickly as possible. The front sight was trained on the sniper's head, lined up with the bill of the gunman's army cap. McCarter squeezed the trigger. The bullet struck a bit low and to the right, but it still hit the intended target. The slug smashed under the gunman's left eye. It splintered the cheekbone and drilled through the skull into the brain.

The sniper released his rifle. It tumbled over the side and clattered to the slate-covered earth below. The assassin clasped both hands to his bullet-shattered face. He quivered in terrible agony for a second or so, but death came quickly. The man's body slumped forward and draped over the rim of the wall, arms dangling lifelessly and blood dripping from the bullet hole in his face.

McCarter turned, pistol ready, looking for the other sniper. He spotted movement along the catwalk and swung the T-51 toward the vague figure. Bullets hammered the support to the minaret closest to McCarter. A ricochet round whistled past his ear. A stone fragment from the pillar stung the side of his skull. McCarter ducked, his head throbbing from the unexpected pain. There was a third sniper on the wall, the Phoenix fighter realized.

Something landed on the platform next to McCarter. He barely had time to register the hand grenade as it rolled near the ladder. The Briton slapped it through the gap, and the grenade plunged inside the tower to the bottom of the minaret. McCarter quickly rose and fired two rounds in the general direction of the third gunman. Then he stepped between the supports and leaped from the minaret.

The grenade exploded. The blast tore apart the base of the tower. A shock wave rode up through the minaret and shook the structure apart. It crashed to earth in a pile of rubble. McCarter heard the minaret collapse thunderously, but even if he had wanted to, he was too busy to take a look.

McCarter had jumped to the roof of the mosque. He landed on the smooth curved dome, arms spread wide in an effort to hug the stone for a handhold that did not exist. He scrabbled with his feet along the surface, and finally the edge of his foot found a narrow ridge at the base of the dome. McCarter clung to the dome, totally exposed to the enemy and barely able to hold on.

A sniper saw the Briton's plight and smiled as he aimed his T-56 at McCarter's back. The Briton still held the pistol in his right hand and slid his left up to the peak of the dome. His fist closed around it, and he managed to find a secure foothold with his other boot. He turned slightly and saw the gunman about to blast him off the mosque.

A volley of automatic fire roared. McCarter flinched and nearly lost his grip on the dome, but none of the bullets were fired in his direction. The sniper spasmed, blood spewing from a wound in the side of his neck. His rifle rose as he fell backward and triggered the weapon. A spray of bullets burst from the T-56 into the sky, then another salvo of automatic fire tore into the sniper's chest and skull.

McCarter glanced down and saw Yakov Katzenelenbogen with the T-50 submachine gun braced across his prosthesis. The Israeli had advanced into the village while McCarter kept the enemy busy. Hsing and Pao had followed, covering the Phoenix commander, yet all held their fire until Katz could get within effective range. The Israeli watched the sniper tumble over the rim and disappear from view.

The third gunman stood, ready to fire at Katz. McCarter in the meantime decided to update himself on the whereabouts of the figure he had seen at the catwalk before the other opponent attacked the minaret. He turned his attention to the enemy's position and saw the killer aiming at Katz. McCarter quickly swung his T-51 pistol toward the assassin and put an extra hole between the buttons of his tunic.

The sniper gasped, startled and hurt by the small-caliber bullet in his chest. McCarter fired three rounds rapid-fire and lodged each slug in the opponent's upper torso. Two bullets pierced the gunman's heart. The man swayed slightly before plunging from the wall.

"That seems to be all of them," Pao declared, returning his pistol to shoulder leather inside his jacket. "Major Hsing tells me his men found another motherless pig in an army Land Rover outside the wall. No doubt they intended to escape in the vehicle.''

"Did they manage to take the fourth man alive?" Katz asked hopefully.

"No," the SAD man answered. "The man opened fire and they had to kill him. Just as we had to kill these three. I should say, you and Masters killed them. The rest of us weren't much help."

"I wouldn't say that, Mr. Pao," Katz assured him, canting the T-50 across a shoulder. "But I wish we'd been able to take a prisoner. So far all we've learned is that the terrorism is even more widespread than we suspected. Which is hardly an encouraging discovery."

"Hey!" McCarter called out as he still clung to the dome of the mosque above. "If it's not asking too bleedin' much, could you blokes try to get a ladder or something so I can get down from here?"

8

"You seem a bit apprehensive, Mr. Vargas," CIA case officer Ross remarked as he watched Rafael Encizo glance out the window of the limo. The Cuban acted as if he expected the car to be ambushed at any moment.

"Being in the capital city of a Communist country does that to me every time," Encizo admitted, switching his gaze from the window to the grim features of SAD agent Yang. "I suppose you're used to it, huh?"

"If that is a joke," Yang replied in a hard flat voice, "then the humor escapes me."

"Forget it," the Cuban said with a shrug. He wished he was sharing the vehicle with Pao instead of Yang, but the former had taken Katz and McCarter to the Hui Region to look into the Islamic revolution theory.

Encizo understood why Pao had decided to investigate personally instead of sending Yang. The lower-ranking SAD agent was too eager to believe the Hui were responsible for the terrorism, which had plagued China. Katz and McCarter were the logical choices to accompany Pao to Ningsia due to their past experience in Islamic countries. Gary Manning had previously mentioned Shanghai as a possible lead, so he and Calvin James had left with a group of SAD agents and soldiers on a flight to the coastal city within minutes after Phoenix Force arrived in Beijing.

John Trent had been taken to the Beijing Militia Police headquarters to interrogate a Japanese tourist. Encizo was not sure why the police were holding the visitor from the Land of the Rising Sun or why SAD thought it was important enough to have Trent assist in the questioning. The centuries-old antagonism between China and Japan might have something to do with it. Perhaps SAD had some reason to suspect the tourist might be a Japanese Red Army terrorist or whatever. Maybe they just wanted to give Trent some sort of busywork to keep an eye on him.

That left Encizo with Ross and Yang to check out the possibility that some of the witnesses of terrorism in Beijing could recall some details that they had failed to report to the authorities earlier. The Cuban considered that kind of effort to be a total waste of time and suspected the SAD had decided to carry out the secondary questioning of witnesses as an excuse to keep the reins on the activities of Phoenix Force and the CIA while they were in China.

Trying to find individuals in a municipal district covering nearly seven thousand square miles and populated by more than eight and a half million people was difficult enough. Many of the witnesses had been street merchants and taxi drivers or tourists who were not the easiest people to locate. Indeed, most of the tourists had already left the country after seeing other visitors killed by terrorists. The few people Yang did interview had nothing to add to their original statement. Encizo did not understand Chinese, so he could do little more than sit in the car and watch.

Yet the journey through the capital was far from dull. Beijing was a fascinating and ancient metropolis. A seat of imperial rule since the Zhou Dynasty, the city had been called many names by different regimes. The Khitan Tartars called it Nanking, the "Southern Capital." Genghis Khan seized the city in 1215 and his grandson, Kublai Khan, later established it as the headquarters of the entire Mongol Empire. Marco Polo wrote of his amazing travels in "Cambaluc." Ming emperors and Manchu rulers of the

Ching Dynasty held court in Beijing. It was the capital of the Chinese republic after the revolution of 1911 and was once again reestablished as the capital after the Communists seized control in 1949.

Beijing was a city with a remarkable history and even more remarkable sites. Encizo had seen the majestic Temple of Heaven when the car passed Tian Tan Park. The temple was enormous, cone-shaped, each of its three sections divided by a massive roof. The crowning pavilion was fit to be a jewel in a god's crown. The intricate designs and skilled craftsmanship were obvious even from a distance.

The famous Forbidden City, a former Imperial Palace of the Manchu emperors, was another unforgettable sight. Ornately carved walls and ramps surrounded the magnificent royal pavilions. Modern colleges and universities were as plentiful as the ancient shrines, temples and palaces. Beijing evidently was the hub of Chinese education. More schools, academies and libraries were located in the capital than any other city in the People's Republic.

And, of course, there were the people. Thousands of people, and every one of them seemed charged with energy and eager to get to whatever task awaited to be dealt with. There seemed to be a national spirit of optimism in China. Perhaps because, after centuries of monarchs and foreign domination, countless wars and revolutions, the repressive tyranny of Chairman Mao, China was changing. Freedoms and opportunities, which had never existed before had started to open up life. The People's Republic was still a long way from true democracy—perhaps it never would be or even *wanted* to be—yet China appeared to be heading in a positive direction.

Encizo wondered if such changes would ever occur in his homeland of Cuba. Would the island nation transform after Fidel Castro's death? Would Rafael Encizo at last be able to go home and visit the site of his parents' house, the foundations of his childhood, cruelly cut short by the Communist persecution, which followed the rise of Castro?

Perhaps anything was possible, but Encizo believed that to be unlikely. Cuba was not China. Castro's regime was virtually an extension of the U.S.S.R. Cuba was not apt to change unless the Soviet Union itself went through a drastic transformation. Encizo had good reason to be cynical of Cuba's future. He had been captured after the Bay of Pigs, held prisoner and tortured. His family had been wiped out by the Communists. These were painful, bitter lessons. Encizo was not apt to forget them because Havana offered deals for better relations with the United States, or the Kremlin boasted of *glasnost* and nuclear disarmament. Encizo considered politicians to be professional liars and found little reassurance in their claims.

The Phoenix pro peered out the rear window of the limo. A blue automobile, similar in design to a Volkswagen Rabbit, weaved around several bicyclists. Encizo was sure he had seen the car before. There were relatively few personal automobiles on the streets of Beijing. As twilight set in, the number of vehicles steadily declined. He was sure it was the same blue car that had been tailing them for the past two hours.

"Yang," he began, "did SAD send some sort of escort car? An unmarked police car or something like that?"

"Why?" the agent asked with a frown.

"Because the car behind us has been following this limo all over town." Encizo turned to Ross. "You know anything about this?"

"Absolutely not," the CIA man assured him. "How about it, Yang? Are those your boys playing follow-the-leader?"

"I know nothing about another car," Yang replied.

"Then let's find out who they are," Encizo suggested. "Are we approaching a large public building of any kind? School, restaurant, hotel, whatever?"

"The Beijing National Library is a few blocks from here," Yang answered. "Why?"

"Tell the driver to head for it," Encizo instructed. "Speed up just a bit. Not too fast. We don't want to make the tail suspicious."

"You're not in any position to give orders," Yang said, his eyes narrowed with anger. "I am in charge here."

"Okay," the Cuban replied with a shrug. "So how do you think we should handle this situation?"

"Somebody think of something," Ross urged.

"Perhaps," Yang began, obviously trying to think of some strategy, but unable to come up with anything fast enough. He reluctantly turned to Encizo. "What is your plan?"

THE LIMOUSINE TURNED the corner and headed for the library. The car slowed slightly and moved closer to the curb. Encizo peered out and saw only a few pedestrians on the sidewalk. He was grateful that "night people" seemed to be a rare species in China. He was also glad he did not see any police in the area.

He turned the handle and pushed the door open, then jumped from the moving vehicle, knees bent to help absorb the impact. Encizo landed on his feet and tumbled into a forward roll. He rode out the fall and ended up near the alley. The limo continued to head toward the library as he ducked into the gap between a small restaurant and a bicycle shop.

Encizo dusted himself off and stood at the mouth of the alley, waiting for the blue car to appear. He did not have to wait long, as just then the vehicle turned the corner and continued to pursue the big black government car. Encizo straightened his jacket's lapels and emerged from the alley, trying to look as nonchalant as possible.

Two elderly Chinese and a teenage girl stared at him with astonishment. The couple had been innocently walking home with their granddaughter when they had seen Encizo's acrobatic performance. They backed away from the Cuban, who smiled and nodded politely.

"Everything's okay," he remarked, uncertain if they understood a word of English. "I asked them to let me off here."

Encizo left the puzzled trio and walked toward the library. The building was roughly three blocks from the alley, and it was difficult to miss. It was easily one of the most magnificent libraries in the entire world. Formerly the Imperial Library under the emperors, it contained more than six million volumes, including works that dated back to the Ming and Sung Dynasties.

The limo parked in front of the library. Yang, Ross and the driver emerged from the car and headed up the great white marble stairs. When the blue car passed the library without even slowing down, Encizo groaned with disappointment. Maybe it had not been tailing them after all.

He kept on in the direction of the library, but he was not looking forward to trying to explain his mistake to Yang and Ross. Hell, the car sure had seemed to be following them. Maybe he was getting paranoid, Encizo was forced to consider. A certain amount of paranoia was healthy in a profession such as his. There was good reason to think somebody might be after him—frequently that was the case. But reasonable and necessary caution could turn to paranoia and emotionally wreck a man. Seeing a threat in every shadow, an enemy in every stranger and constant suspicion of circumstances had ruined more than one operative involved in high-risk covert missions.

Then Encizo spotted the blue car. It had parked about half a block from the library. The vehicle had pulled up to a curb in front of a parked tour bus. Cute stunt, Encizo acknowledged. The bus would conceal the blue car from the view of Yang, Ross and the driver when they left the library. Then the driver would simply wait for the limo to move again and continue to pursue it.

Encizo strolled to the rear of the bus, his manner neither rushed nor stealthful. He wished he was armed, but Yang had refused to loan him a weapon. Encizo wanted to know how many passengers were in the blue car and have some notion about who they might be. Most terrorists were a desperate bunch and needed little excuse to draw weapons and start shooting. Some of the worst fanatics would not hesitate to pull the pin from a grenade or set off a bomb even if it meant they had to commit suicide in order to kill an opponent.

The Cuban walked alongside the bus, approaching from the driver's side. He hoped whoever was in the blue car was paying a lot more attention to the library than the surroundings. Encizo drew closer and cast a quick glance into the back window. There were only two men inside. One had unfolded a map, probably one of the city, while the other rolled down the window and lighted a cigarette.

The fellow with the map put it down and opened the door on the passenger side. He stepped from the vehicle. The man was over six feet tall, well built and dressed in a European-style suit and tie. A cloth cap was pulled down low on his brow, but Encizo saw blond hair beneath the back of the hat. Whoever he was, for sure he was not Chinese.

The man headed toward the library. His companion remained in the car, seated behind the steering wheel. Encizo walked to the driver's side. Cigarette smoke drifted from the open window. The man in the car suddenly noticed Encizo and jerked in his seat. His hand moved inside his suit jacket.

"Hi," Encizo greeted with a smile. "You American? Speak English, friend?"

The man tossed his cigarette out the window and glared at Encizo. His manner of dressing was the same as his companion's, but he appeared to be a bit shorter and more stocky. His hair was black and his features appeared to be Eurasian.

"You know how to get to the tourist information center from here?" Encizo inquired.

"No speak English," the man replied, shaking his head.

"Oh," Encizo said with a nod as he pushed back the coattails of his jacket and moved his hand to the small of his back. "Then you don't know that I'm about to shoot you in the head, do you?"

The man's eyes widened with fear, and he thrust his hand inside his jacket once again. Encizo's right fist rocketed through the open window and slammed into the man's face. He grabbed the man's coat sleeve and tugged at the arm until it was hauled from inside the jacket, along with a blue-black pistol, similar in size and design to a Walther PPK.

"Cristo!" Encizo exclaimed as he quickly grabbed the man's wrist with both hands.

He weaved away from the muzzle of the gun as he pulled the man's arm through the open window. His opponent struggled and tried to force the pistol toward the Cuban's chest, but Encizo held the arm fast. The man reached forward with his free hand to claw at Encizo's head.

Encizo ignored the stinging pain in his scalp and slammed the man's arm across the car door. With a groan, the opponent allowed his hand to open and the pistol fell from his hold. Encizo pulled on the captive limb, raised it and smashed the forearm across the unyielding metal. Bone cracked and the man howled. Encizo struck the broken limb across the door a third time. His opponent uttered a whimpering gasp and passed out.

The blond man let out a bellow as he ran back to the car to help his distressed comrade.

Encizo quickly scooped up the fallen pistol. He recognized it immediately. A Russian 9 mm Makarov. The Cuban saw the second opponent leap forward and land on the trunk of the car. Heedless or unaware of the gun in Encizo's fist, he launched himself at the Cuban like a pouncing leopard.

The Phoenix pro held his fire. He was reluctant to shoot an unarmed man under any circumstances, and he also wanted to take the man alive, if at all possible. Encizo tried to sidestep, but the enemy crashed into him like a sandbag dropped from a second-story window.

The impact drove both of them to the pavement, with Encizo underneath. He felt the breath driven from his lungs, and his head kissed the sidewalk hard. His larger and younger opponent grabbed the Cuban's forearm and slapped it into the concrete to jar the pistol from his grasp. The gun skidded across the pavement, but Encizo swung a hard punch with his left hand.

The big man grunted. Encizo planted a foot in his stomach and shoved hard. That managed to free him. He climbed to his feet, but the blond opponent delivered another charge. Head down like a bull, the man lunged and rammed his hard cranium into Encizo's stomach. The charge drove Encizo back against the frame of the car. He felt as if he might throw up, but he still hammered the bottom of his fist across his opponent's bowed neck. Gritting his teeth against the nausea, he thought, okay, Blondie, this is it.

Then he whipped a knee under Blondie's jaw. The blow straightened the man's back and his head bounced, then teeth clashing together hard. But he was a tough son of a bitch and swung a wild right cross at Encizo's head. The Cuban raised his left forearm to block the punch, then drove his right fist into the other man's solar plexus.

Blondie staggered from the blow. Encizo's left arm swung over his opponent's right and clasped the man's forearm under his armpit. He locked the grip and rammed a right uppercut to the solar plexus again. Gasping, the man doubled up from the blow. Encizo followed up with a short punch to the chin. Blood oozed from Blondie's mouth, but he still grabbed the Cuban's right wrist with his free hand.

Encizo immediately lashed a kick to the groin. The man howled in agony and released Encizo. He staggered backward, knees bent crookedly, both hands attempting to quell the pain. His mouth hung open in a black oval, and his eyes were squeezed shut. Encizo hit him, putting all his weight behind the punch. The blond man folded into a heap on the sidewalk.

"Vargas!" Ross called as he jogged toward Encizo. "You all right?"

"I could use an aspirin and a bowl of ice," the Cuban replied, rubbing a bruised knuckle. "But I'm okay."

"You did not tell us you would do anything like this," Yang commented as he appeared next to Ross and glanced down at the unconscious man. "Is he dead?"

"No, but he might sing soprano for a while," Encizo remarked and gathered up the Makarov pistol. He handed it butt-first to Yang. "The guy in the car had this. Recognize it?"

"It is a Russian side arm," Yang said with surprise.

"Yeah," Encizo confirmed. "And my guess is these guys are made in the U.S.S.R. as well. It'll be interesting to hear what they've got to say about this."

9

Ming Ssu entered the *kwoon*. The training hall was devoted to practice of *wu shu*—martial arts. The former SAD spy watched some young men being instructed in fundamental stance, blocking techniques and striking. The *sifu* instructor barked numbers and swung his arms into a block-hit combination. The students stood in the "horse-straddled" stance and repeated each technique displayed by the *sifu*.

More advanced students engaged in free-spare. They threw rapid punches and kicks at one another. Battle cries filled the hall as the combatants tried to parry, block or dodge attacks and counter with hand and foot strokes of their own. Hands chopped air, sleeves snapped as fists shot forward, and arched fingers struck out like animal claws. There was a flashing of legs, and opponents ducked and weaved to dodge attacks and attempt to counterattack. Referees watched the mock battles with care to be certain no one was injured during practice.

Ming was not sure what style they were trained in. *Tz-men, yung-ch'un chuan* or one of the other martial arts popular in Mainland China. Probably combinations of techniques from more than one form. There were literally hundreds of different Chinese martial arts. Westerners tended to lump these together as "kung fu," which was actually a term meaning "work," "skill," "exercise" or "training" rather than an actual martial arts form. Ming had never put much stock in unarmed combat of any kind. Punches and kicks were no match for bullets.

Commander Kuo Chun was engaged in the training, sparring with a male opponent. Both were armed with halberds. The weapons were wooden training tools, of course, since the sparring practice with real halberds would be too dangerous. Some real halberds were mounted in a weapons rack with spears, swords and other traditional *wu shu* weapons. Large, polished swordlike blades mounted on seven-foot poles, halberds had been devastating weapons before firearms and cannons made them obsolete.

But Kuo wielded the wooden halberd as if the weapon still served a useful purpose on battlefields. She lashed out at her opponent with almost frenzied fury, driving back the male trainee with a series of forceful, if rather graceless strokes. Kuo was involved in physical training with the same fanatic passion as politics. Once again, Mao Tse-tung was her inspiration. Mao's first published article had been *A Study of Physical Culture* in 1917. He had stressed that the most strenuous form of exercise should be pursued because the main purpose of "physical education is military heroism."

Kuo had followed the teachings of Mao with absolute dedication. Years of hard exercise had given her broad shoulders, big biceps and heavily muscled legs that would have seemed more appropriate for the physique of a man. Kuo had little concerns with being a woman, and her male comrades soon barely noticed she was one.

The commander hammered the wooden blade of her halberd across the shaft of her opponent's weapon as he held it overhead like a bar. The man looked as if he was afraid she might crack his skull with one of those vicious blows. The fear was well founded, as Kuo had broken bones during numerous training bouts in the past.

She suddenly raised her weapon and struck with the butt end of the pole. The stroke was similar to a trick shot by a pool player with a cue stick. The pole jabbed the man hard in the stomach. He doubled up with a gasp of pain, and Kuo chopped the dull part of the blade across his collarbone. He fell to the mat, moaning and grasping at fractured bone between shoulder and neck.

A first-aid specialist hurried to the fallen man and muttered something under his breath, possibly a comment about Kuo's unnecessary brutality. But the commander paid little attention to her defeated opponent or the medic. She had seen Ming and approached him, her halberd canted across her shoulder. Ming Ssu wished he could be somewhere else and meeting with just about anyone instead of Commander Kuo at that moment.

"Comrade Ming," she began with a formal nod. "You bring good news of our campaign in Ningsia?"

"I regret to inform the Comrade Commander that our operation in the Hui Region has been less than successful," Ming reluctantly admitted.

"You mean you failed?" Kuo snapped, glaring at him as she gripped the shaft of her halberd so hard her knuckles turned white from the stress.

"Everything was executed according to plan," Ming insisted. "In fact, circumstances seemed most favorable. Two military vehicles were reported in the area. Four soldiers with a government official in civilian clothing and two Occidental visitors. When they approached a small farming community, it seemed an ideal opportunity to carry out the strike. Some Hui villagers would be killed, the army and the government would naturally be blamed for the incident and possibly CIA involvement could be worked into the propaganda concerning the event."

"What went wrong?" Kuo demanded.

"Our men were killed," Ming answered. "All four of them. I'm not certain what happened. They probably continued the attack too long instead of striking and pulling out immediately. The soldiers must have gotten the upper hand somehow and wiped out the assault team."

"You did not prepare for the possibility the soldiers would fight our comrades?" Kuo hissed as she threw the halberd aside, perhaps because she was too tempted to use it on Ming. "Chairman Mao warned to fight no battle unprepared, and fight no battle you are not certain of winning!"

"Then Chairman Mao would have us fight no battles at all!" Ming snapped in reply, disgusted by Kuo's attitude that Mao was an infallible source of all knowledge. "There is *always* a risk of losing in combat. It is impossible to be certain of winning every battle. You can win *fan-tan* nine games in a row, but that does not mean you won't lose the tenth."

"I speak of battlefield victories and you talk of gamblers' folly," Kuo spat angrily. "Our revolution is at stake. You were responsible for the Ningsia campaign, and I hold you to account for this failure."

"Do you intend to take me outside and shoot me?" Ming asked with a shrug. "I suppose you can do that, but it won't change anything. The situation appeared perfect for our needs. My intelligence sources confirmed that there were only four soldiers and an official from Beijing with two white foreigners. There was no reason to suspect anything would go wrong, but the unexpected came into play. It is that simple. Besides, it isn't the disaster you say it is. None of our comrades were captured. They are dead, and they can't tell our enemies anything about us. All were dressed in Chinese army uniforms with Chinese army weapons. We can still turn the incident into a propaganda victory against the army and the government. Several Hui

Muslims were killed. Those deaths can still be blamed on the military. We'll claim SAD and CIA ordered the men to be killed to cover up their own part in the atrocity.''

"It might work," Kuo admitted, her anger subsiding. "You had better see that it does, Comrade."

"I'll do my best," Ming promised.

"Something wrong?" Carlton Neville inquired as he approached Kuo and Ming.

The two Chinese turned to face Neville, although they would have been glad never to set eyes on the renegade British mercenary again. Neville was a forty-two-year-old, ex-British army officer who had quit the service to become a soldier of fortune. He fought in several mercenary armies in four different African countries, often switching sides if a better offer and money were available.

The tall, dignified Englishman with a salt-and-pepper mustache and a bit of gray at his temples was a cold-blooded killer and an opportunist. Neville got involved in the Golden Triangle opium business in the late 1970s. His association with Feng's Red Fist Tong led to his current role with the New Guard. Neither Kuo nor Ming liked working with Neville, but he served a useful purpose in their plan.

"Private conversation?" Neville asked. He spoke Singapore Chinese—a Cantonese dialect—with a smattering of Mandarin, but he knew they understood him. "We can talk later if you like."

"What do you want to talk about?" Kuo demanded, glancing at the .45 Colt pistol holstered on Neville's hip.

She noticed Paul Gowers and Craig Kelly standing by the entrance. Gowers was a short man with curly red hair and a square-shaped face with surprisingly delicate features. Kelly was a big black bruiser, a former dope pusher in his hometown of Detroit.

The two Americans had teamed up in Saigon, dealing Vietnamese syndicate heroin to U.S. troops. When CID busted some of their customers, Gowers and Kelly knew they would get the ax next. Those junkies were bound to squeal when the pigs put the squeeze on them. The pushers deserted before the Green Machine could nail them.

They had been doing business with the Golden Triangle Triad syndicates in Thailand. Sometimes they sold dope to Occidental tourists in Bangkok and Songkhla. Sometimes they traveled to Australia, delivering shipments of white powder to the syndicates down under. From time to time, the Triad wanted someone killed, and Gowers and Kelly were always willing to accept a contract if the price was right.

Commander Kuo was not certain how the American deserters and the British merc had become associated with the Red Fist Tong. She did not care as long as the foreigners did as they were told. Most likely she would have them executed after they were no longer useful. Kuo was still debating that decision. Feng would also be expendable, although there might be need for his tong in the future. Time would reveal where to trim the excess from her personnel, and she would decide what to do then.

"The other chaps and I would like to know when we'll get our money for the Shanghai hit," Neville told Kuo. "You must admit it went smoothly. We did our job exactly as you ordered. No reason for complaints. Correct?"

"Your work was satisfactory," Kuo replied.

"I'm so glad," the mercenary remarked. "The price was five hundred thousand Hong Kong dollars. We'll take Australian dollars, Japanese yen, Thai bahts, Indian rupees, or gold. Just about anything except Chinese yuan. We really don't want to advertise that we were in the People's Republic when we move to our new destination."

"You talk as if you plan to leave soon," Ming remarked.

"We've finished our part," Neville stated. "Mission accomplished. Your little revolution isn't our concern now. Unless you want to contract us for more assignments before we leave. Naturally our fee will be higher..."

"You will get your money, Mr. Neville," Kuo snapped. "We may indeed have more work for you. If you're interested."

"How long will we have to stay?" the mercenary asked.

"Three days," the terrorist leader replied. "Perhaps five. You will be paid an additional one hundred thousand Hong Kong dollars for your time, and five hundred thousand if you participate in another operation. This is fair. Agreed?"

"I'll talk to Feng and the two Yanks," Neville stated. "It sounds like a good deal to me. If they agree, we'll stay."

"See to it," Kuo told him with a curt nod.

Neville bowed in reply and turned to walk for the door. The two Americans followed the merc, asking him questions in English. Kuo waited until they were gone and spat on the floor where Neville had stood. Ming grunted in agreement.

"Disgusting to have to work with a *wang-pu-tan* like that," Ming muttered.

"Consider it a sacrifice for our cause," Kuo said with a sigh. "You will see what you can do about the propaganda campaign?"

"Of course," the former SAD agent confirmed. "I'm also getting some intelligence concerning flights arriving from the United States and Western Europe. We already have a list of tours popular with Occidental tourists. Time, location and even a fair knowledge of the number of individuals to expect on each day of the week."

"There may be greater security at these sites," Kuo warned.

Ming nodded sagely. "No doubt about that. There will be more police and probably Social Affairs Department personnel watching for potential trouble. It is even possible the army may have troops in the area of popular tourist attractions, but I doubt they will be too close, because armed troops are not the image Beijing wants to present to foreign visitors."

"There are hundreds of historic landmarks in China," Kuo commented. "How do we decide which site will be most vulnerable?"

"The one that will be the most difficult to protect," Ming answered. "And I know which one that is. A popular site which the authorities cannot possibly secure against attack. A target which will allow us to slaughter hundreds of Occidental trash, and no one will be able to stop us."

10

Calvin James slipped into the harness of his Jackass Leather shoulder holster rig. He clipped the sheath to the Jet Aer G-96 fighting dagger under his right arm. The handle of the knife hung upside down, thumb break to the sheath within easy reach. James smiled as he picked up his Beretta 92-F and worked the slide to chamber the first round.

"I feel better already," the black warrior remarked as he switched the pistol to safety mode and slipped it into the holster under his left arm.

"It does feel good to have personal weapons back," Gary Manning admitted. The Canadian sat at the conference table, Walther P-5 in shoulder leather under his arm. He had a disassembled FAL assault rifle on the table and slid a cleaning rod through the barrel as he spoke. "I guess this means Mr. Pao has decided we can be trusted after all."

"Your friends Gray and Masters convinced us during the firefight at the Hui village," Major Hsing stated. "They proved they are not working with the terrorists. They also displayed remarkable skill and courage during the battle."

"They said the same thing about you, Major," James replied. He opened a long aluminum case and removed an M-16 rifle. "They told us you risked your life to save a wounded man. Bullets were coming down like raindrops, but you didn't back off."

"I am a soldier," Hsing replied, trying to conceal his pleasure at such praise. "I simply did what is expected of me."

"Hey," James said, breaking open his M-16 to check the barrel. "They don't issue a man stainless steel balls with an army uniform. If you want to be modest, that's okay. Where's everybody else? We just get back from Shanghai, and Masters and Gray told us briefly about the incident in Ningsia and sent us here to get our weapons. Everybody else go out for late dinner or something?"

"I'm not sure," Hsing admitted. "Mr. Pao told me to have your belongings ready for all of you. Then he met with Yang. I haven't seen him since, but I believe he took Gray and Masters to another part of the building. Perhaps to the interrogation section."

"Interrogation?" Manning asked with surprise. "I thought you guys didn't take any prisoners at Ningsia."

"We didn't," Hsing confirmed, "but apparently Yang and your friend Vargas *did*."

There was a heavy knock at the door, accompanied by McCarter's unmistakable East London voice. "Open up, mates," he urged. "Need to talk to Johnson on the double."

Hsing opened the door. The Briton entered. He grinned at his teammates when he saw they were once again armed with familiar weapons and he patted his jacket. The Browning Hi-Power was back in its usual place under his arm.

"I know just how you feel," the British ace declared. "Johnson, get your scopolamine and whatever else you'll need. We've got a couple blokes in detention who've been reluctant to answer questions. Might need your expertise with truth serum."

"You got it," James answered, putting down his rifle to grab a case filled with medical equipment. "These the guys Vargas caught?"

"Rumors fly around here," McCarter remarked. "They were following Vargas and Yang all over Beijing this evening. Pretty sure they're Russians. Probably KGB."

"Holy shit," James rasped. "I'm comin'."

John Trent appeared at the doorway behind McCarter. The Briton moved to let the American ninja enter as James headed for the door. Trent watched him bolt into the hall with McCarter.

"Something must have happened," Trent remarked. He turned to Manning for an answer.

"I'll fill you in while you get your gear," the Canadian explained. "I heard you were at the police militia headquarters interrogating somebody."

"Yes," Trent muttered with disgust as he searched through the luggage for his cases. "A Japanese tourist got lost around the Mao Tse-tung Memorial Museum. Some idiot thought he might be a terrorist or a Kompei spy or something. I spent hours talking with the poor fellow, and even more time with the police and the cretin SAD saddled me with. It was all nonsense, but it's over now."

He opened the latch to a long aluminum case which Hsing had assumed contained another assault rifle. The major was startled when Trent removed a three-and-a-half-foot sword in a black scabbard from the case. The hilt was wrapped in sharkskin and twisted silk, which suggested it was Japanese, yet the scabbard was straight, which meant the blade was not curved like that of a traditional samurai sword. The handguard was large, square and black.

Major Hsing recalled Japanese swords he had seen in books and museum display. The *katana* of the samurai had been an elegant weapon, a work of art with an ornate *tsuba* handguard, bearing the family crest and a symbolic reminder of *bushido*, code of honor. But "Timothy Carson's" sword was not fancy, expensive or decorative. It was a functional tool, not a work of art or a family antique.

"Do you really think you'll have an occasion to use that?" Hsing asked with a baffled look. The world was approaching the 21st Century. It seemed incredible to him that anyone would still regard a sword as a serious combat weapon.

"Such occasions have occurred in the past," Trent replied simply as he placed the sword on the table.

THE STOCKY MAN sat rigidly in the chair. His broken arm was supported by a sling tied to his neck. He cradled the injured limb gingerly to his chest with his other arm and squinted to shield his eyes from the bright lamp trained directly on his face. The man sweated freely, more from tension than the heat of the light, and his black hair was plastered to his forehead.

"Dobri v'yeh-chyer," Yakov Katzenelenbogen greeted. He stood in the shadows beyond the lamp. "We can talk in Russian if you like, or English. My associate, Mr. Vargas, told me you understood when he said he was going to shoot you."

"Ich verstehe nicht!" the man replied. *"Ich bin Deutscher!"*

"Sehr gut!" Katz declared. "I speak German as well. You pick whatever language you wish, but you'd better start answering some questions. Why were you following the limo?"

"We followed no one," the Russian answered. "We were simply going in the same direction."

"Why did you pull a gun when Mr. Vargas spoke to you by your car?" Katz asked. "A Soviet-made Makarov. A silencer for the pistol was also found in your pocket. Now, do you really expect us to believe you're a tourist from the Federal Republic of Germany?''

"You have my passport," the man replied.

"Ja." Katz chuckled. "I have a fake passport myself. We'll use scopolamine if we have to. Truth serum can be dangerous, you know. Terrible strain on the heart."

"I demand to call the German embassy," the prisoner declared.

"You're not getting anything until you answer some questions," Katz informed him. "I'm afraid things aren't going to be very pleasant for you."

Calvin James entered the interrogation room. Pao was already in the room with Katz and the prisoner. James opened his bag and removed a stethoscope and mercury sphygmomanometer.

"Okay," James began. "First I'm gonna check his heart and blood pressure. If I decide it would kill him to give the guy a dose of scopolamine, I won't use the drug. If you SAD dudes don't like it, get somebody else to give him truth serum instead. I'm not gonna give a man a heart attack because there's a vague chance he might wheeze out an answer or two before he takes his final gasp."

"Mr. Gray assures me you have a great deal of experience at this," Pao replied. "We will honor your decision."

"Great," James said with a nod. "Now, do you fellas have a polygraph machine around here?"

"A lie detector?" Pao frowned. "Those machines are unreliable. Is it not true that people have been known to lie without being detected by a polygraph, and innocent people appear to be lying due to the stress level registered on the machine?"

"The polygraph is not much use as a lie detector," James agreed, "but it does a nice job of tracking a person's heart, blood pressure and stress level. If I give scopolamine, I want to be able to monitor all that stuff. I want to see if the drug is too hard on his metabolism. If it looks like he's about to blow a heart valve, I can give him a sedative and try to counter the effects. I also want to see if he's trying to fight the effects of the drug. It is possible, although very unlikely, to lie under the influence of scopolamine, but there's no way he could do it and beat the polygraph at the same time."

"What about a posthypnotic response to scopolamine?" Pao asked. "Some agents undergo such posthypnotic training as a defense from truth serums. The drug would simply trigger a subconscious cover story from the man's mind."

"You SAD agents do keep up with things," James commented. "Once again, the polygraph would catch that. A person is very relaxed when hypnotized. If the stress level is too low, then we'll know he's had posthypnotic conditioning."

"Sounds like you cover everything," Pao remarked, impressed by the black man's knowledge.

"We try," James assured him. "Interrogation should be done in the subject's native language, of course. Do you know what that is, Gray?"

"He claims he's German," Katz answered, "but he has a Slavic accent. Belorussian is my guess. Fellow was probably born in or near Minsk. I'll interrogate him in Russian after you give him the drug."

"So let's get to it," James declared.

RAFAEL ENCIZO and CIA case officer Ross joined Manning, McCarter and Trent in the conference room. Major Hsing had some food delivered. Surprisingly the SAD headquarters had an all-night kitchen in the building. Perhaps not so surprising, considering the nature and history of the Chinese intelligence service.

The Chinese, perhaps more than any other culture, have traditionally viewed espionage as a necessary activity, and those who conduct intelligence operations are regarded with respect and honor. The West tends to consider espionage as "dirty business" and spies as "sneaks and liars." Aside from the romance of James Bond fiction, secret agents have generally been regarded as amoral, cold-blooded sociopaths. Even the Soviet Union tends to view the KGB with fear rather than respect.

To the Chinese, however, spying is a very old and honorable profession. The agent is considered a patriot, willing to take great risks and make many sacrifices for his country. Sun Tzu, author of *Principles of War*, warned that intelligence was vital to the security of a nation during peacetime, as well as times of war. He claimed that the failure to treat espionage agents with rewards and honors was "the height of inhumanity."

An all-night kitchen was hardly remarkable when it served the interests and needs of the Social Affairs Department. Pao and Yang had no trouble getting automobiles, assistance from the military or cooperation from the local police. The lessons of Sun Tzu had been well learned and, nearly three thousand years later, were still followed in China.

The meal was agreeable enough: boiled chicken, with noodles, cashews, fried rice and assorted vegetables. Coffee—a surprising rich blend recently imported from Indonesia—was offered as well as tea. They even had a chilled bottle of Coca Cola for McCarter. However, the waiting became tedious after three hours. At last Katz, James and Pao returned to the room and joined the others.

"Jesus, it's about time," Ross complained.

"You think we had more fun down there in interrogation than you did?" James said, tired and irritable. "You can forget that, jack."

"Did you get them to talk?" Encizo inquired, eager to hear about the two men he had captured virtually single-handedly.

"Oh, yes," Katz replied, lowering himself into a chair. "They are KGB, as we suspected. We've got their real names, the names of their control agents in Macao, details about how they entered China and all that rot on tape. They were following the limousine because they knew it was a government vehicle, and sorry, Ross..."

"They know I'm CIA?" Ross asked, already aware of the answer. "Well, hell. My cover is sure blown to hell. First SAD, now KGB. What's next? A television documentary about my screwed up career?"

"You've still got a career," Katz assured him, "but you'll certainly be transferred from the Far East after this assignment. At any rate, KGB decided to tail the limo because they hoped to find evidence of misadventures to implicate SAD or CIA as being responsible for the terrorism in China. Apparently someone in the Kremlin was counting on latching on to something to denounce either the United States or the People's Republic or both."

"In other words," Manning began with a sigh, "KGB doesn't know squat about who is responsible for the terrorist activities."

"Are you sure they're telling the truth?" Ross asked.

"Yeah," James assured him. "Both had scopolamine, and we questioned them separately, compared their answers to see if they agreed and questioned them again just to be sure. Those Russkies don't know as much about this as we do, and we still know nothing."

"Well, I suggest we all get some sleep," Katz announced. "It's been a long day and tomorrow promises to be even longer."

11

The traffic in Shanghai was heavy that morning. Yet the bustle on the streets in terms of vehicles was far less than most Westerners would have expected in one of the largest cities in the world, and in fact the largest in Mainland China, with a population of nearly twelve million people.

Calvin James and John Trent walked among the enormous crowds of pedestrians. The pair would have been a novelty ten years earlier, and fifteen years previously they would have shocked onlookers. Twenty-five years ago they would have been seized by the authorities. However, the Chinese in Shanghai were now accustomed to foreigners in their streets. Tourists, businessmen and visiting dignitaries were a familiar sight in the city.

It was hard to believe Shanghai had simply been a fishing village in the 11th Century. It had become a center of industry, commercial trade and transportation. Shanghai was the major port city for all of China. Manufacturing of textiles, steel and electrical equipment thrived in Shanghai. Shipbuilding was another important trade. Petroleum refining, publishing and chemical processing were among the other main businesses, which made Shanghai a vital and still-growing city.

James and Trent saw little of the big businesses as they roamed the streets. The Phoenix pro from Chicago had to rely on Trent's expertise in Mandarin Chinese to ask for directions to get to their destination. James was not even sure where they were going, and he only hoped Trent was as fluent in the language as he seemed to be.

"We're almost there," Trent announced after he spoke with a merchant in a street shop. He handed James a pair of black chopsticks with gold dragons engraved in the wood. "I bought two pair. One for you and one for me. Mementos of Shanghai."

"You shouldn't have," James remarked dryly.

"The shopkeeper insisted I buy something," Trent explained. "He wanted fifty yuan for the chopsticks, along with the information. Naturally I haggled with him. Got the price down to thirty yuan."

"I just hope he gave you the right directions," James commented as they continued to stroll through the streets. He noticed a small tower in the center of the street, a metal hut with glass windows atop a stalk of steel girders. Two uniformed figures were inside the tower. "Hey, what's that thing?"

"Traffic cops," Trent answered. "They figure they can see the traffic better from an elevated perch in the middle of the street. It seems to work all right, but they don't have the sort of traffic problems here as they have in the States."

"Yeah," James agreed, watching several figures pedal past the police post on bikes. "What's the name of the place we're headed?"

"*Yun-chi Ba,*" Trent replied. "The 'Lucky Egg.' Don't be deceived by the cute name. My uncle tells me it's a den of thieves. There are men at the Lucky Egg who will cut your throat for the money in your pockets."

"So you mentioned earlier," James commented, wondering if they should have stayed in Beijing. "I hope this pans out. Hate to get my throat cut following a false lead."

Trent simply shrugged in reply. They were pursuing a long shot, and they both knew it. Trent had intended to come alone, but the others insisted he was being foolhardy so he reluctantly agreed to take James. The black man did not look like the type of person most Chinese would associate with an American law enforcement officer or CIA. The SAD, police and military would be spotted before they got within two blocks of the *Yun-chi Ba*. The crime syndicates in Mainland China had survived the oppression of Mao Tse-tung's government and it was more demanding than usual to run illegal trade under a totalitarian regime. They had not been successful for so long because they were careless.

James and Trent continued to walk through the crowds in the streets. Occasionally they saw other foreigners among the sea of faces. Tourists, mostly Americans, and business executives, who seemed to be European, hustled through the streets of Shanghai. Taxicabs tried to keep up with the visitors. The number of cabs in China had increased dramatically since the new reforms after Mao's death. Taxi drivers had become model examples of creeping capitalism in the People's Republic.

"Hey, Mees-tir!" a cabbie called out in Pidgin English. "Where you want to go? I take in cab. You go there many quick. I know fun place in Shanghai. Many fun place."

"I think I met this guy in Tijuana," James muttered.

"Fun place later," Trent replied. "Business first."

As last they approached the Lucky Egg. It was one of several seedy-looking taverns near the main port of the Hangpu River, the vital waterway linking Shanghai with the Yangtze River inland, as well as the East China Sea. The *Yun-chi Ba* was easy to recognize, although James did not understand the ideographs written across the oval sign above the door. The sign was in the shape of a giant egg.

They pushed through the beaded curtain at the door and entered the dark, stale-smelling tavern. A fat Chinese sat on a stool behind the bar. Two younger men, clad in black shirts, trousers and sandals hurried from a table to meet the visitors.

"We close now," one of them announced. "No open three o'clock."

"Ch'ing, ch'ing," Trent replied, smoothly slipping into rapid Mandarin. "We need to speak to Mr. Hong. Private business."

"I know no one named Mr. Hong," the man stated. "You have come to the wrong place."

"We have associates in the Red Eyebrow Society in the United States of America," Trent explained. "A city called San Francisco. Please, give Mr. Hong this."

Trent took a copper coin from his pocket and handed it to the man. He examined it with surprise, recognizing the ideograms for fire, water, wind and earth. He closed his fist around the coin.

"Wait a minute," the man urged with a short bow.

"Shi'eh, shi'eh," Trent thanked him and bowed in reply.

The man hurried across the barroom while his companion stood beside the strangers. The tavern was quiet, virtually deserted except for James, Trent, the bartender and the flunky with them. Less than a minute later, the man returned and gestured for Trent and James to follow him.

The pair were led to a room at the back of the bar. The youth opened the door and indicated that James and Trent were to enter. They stepped up to the threshold. Three men waited for them in the storage room within. Two were armed with knives, and the third had a short club in his fist.

"Shit!" James exclaimed as he whirled and swung the back of his fist to the face of the punk who had tried to set them up.

The youth cried out and fell heavily. A knife slipped from his fingers and skidded across the floor. The three hoods in the storage room bellowed a battle cry in unison and charged. Trent swiftly took a small, egg-shaped object from his coat pocket and hurled it at the floor near their feet. The *metsubushi* exploded on impact. Flash powder burst in a blinding glare of white light, and black powder rose in a cloud into the faces of the three attackers.

Blinded by the flash and choking on pepper, one of the knife artists still lunged. Trent easily dodged the attack and grabbed the wrist above the man's knife. James kicked the man in the abdomen as Trent wrenched the wrist forcibly to force the opponent to drop his blade. Trent glimpsed the club-wielding thug charging through the doorway with his cudgel raised. The American ninja pushed his disarmed opponent into the path of the other man who, still half-blind, lashed out with his weapon and slammed it across the skull of his own comrade.

The man moaned and slumped to the floor as the enraged club-swinger attacked again. The American ninja jumped back and pulled something from his hip pocket. It was a *manrikigusari*, a two and a half foot long fighting chain with a weight on each end. Trent slashed the *manrikigusari* in a fast figure-eight pattern. The man with the blunt object dodged the first swipe, but the chain swung in a high arc and a weighted end clipped him on the side of the skull.

The second knife artist blinked his eyes and spit, trying to clear his vision and shake off the effects of the black powder. He hissed at Calvin James and lunged through the doorway of the storage room. James gripped the open door, waited a split second and slammed it into his attacker. The door vibrated from the impact of the hood running into it. James heard a groan and pulled back the door. The knife artist staggered backward, blade in his fist, eyes glazed. Blood oozed from his broken nose.

James stepped forward and adroitly kicked the knife from his opponent's hand. His right hand plowed into the man's solar plexus, and his left hooked him in the jaw. The man fell into a stack of crates and dropped senseless to the floor.

James turned to see a figure leap forward. Something flashed through the air, and a sandal-clad foot slammed into the side of James's face. He fell back against a wall, head ringing from the kick. The one who had led them to the storage room closed in and drove a fist into James's belly. He raised his hand, prepared to follow the attack with a chop to the black man's neck.

The Phoenix commando quickly blocked the blow with his left forearm. The hood's wrist struck the black man's sturdy limb, and he hissed from the sharp pain to the ulnar nerve. James thrust with an underhand stab, his fingers rigid like the blades of four knives. The hard tips stabbed the Chinese attacker under the rib cage. The opponent gasped breathlessly and started to double up. James bent an elbow and whipped it under the jawbone in an uppercut *empi* stroke.

The man tumbled against the doorway. His skull rapped the wooden framework, and blood dripped from his lips. James hooked a kick under his opponent's ribs, aiming for the same spot where he had delivered the spear-hand thrust before. The thug moaned and folded at the waist, both arms clutching his belly. James brought his fist down like a hammer between the man's shoulder blades, and the Asian fell facedown on the floor, sighed feebly and passed out.

John Trent still had his hands full as well. The club-wielding hoodlum remained on his feet, determined to bash in the skull of the American ninja. Worse, the bartender and the other flunky in the barroom were also headed toward the back of the tavern to assist their criminal colleagues.

The brute with the club swung his weapon once more. Trent raised the *manrikigusari*, a weighted end in each fist, the chain held taunt like a solid bar. The club struck the steel links and bounced off. Trent quickly snap-kicked his opponent in the lower abdomen and adroitly wrapped the chain around the club. A hard tug ripped the cudgel from the man's grasp and sent it hurtling to the floor. Trent's fists lashed out like twin hammers and struck the metal ends of the *manrikigusari* into the forehead of his opponent. The man dropped to the floor.

"Hold it!" James snapped, drawing the Beretta 92-F from shoulder leather. He pointed it at the two remaining opponents. "Kung Fu Theater is over. You guys want to see *Gunfight at the OK Corral* next?"

They may not have understood a word James said, but there was no mistaking the meaning of the gun pointed at their bellies. The bartender and his companion dropped their weapons—a short club and a dagger—and raised their hands. Trent put away his fighting chain and shook his head sadly.

"I guess this idea didn't work out too well," he remarked.

"Doesn't look like it," James agreed. "Let's get the hell out of here."

He started to return his Beretta to its holster when another door across from the storage room opened. James swung the pistol toward the door as a small, elderly Chinese stepped from the room. He wore a white silk shirt with a Mandarin collar, baggy black trousers and a Rolex wristwatch. The old man looked at the gun as calmly as if James were pointing a blue-black cucumber at his chest.

"What is going on here?" he demanded curtly in English. He repeated the question in rapid-fire Chinese.

"Mr. Hong?" Trent inquired.

"Perhaps," the old man replied. "What do you want?"

"We wish to talk to you, Mr. Hong," Trent stated.

"You seem to talk with your fists," Hong remarked, glancing at the unconscious bodies scattered about the floor.

"They set us up," James insisted as he slipped his pistol back inside his jacket. "We went easy on them, too. If we hadn't, you'd have six fresh corpses out here."

"You may well speak the truth," Hong admitted, and there was a trace of amusement in his expression. "You wish to talk with me? Then we shall talk."

A TELEPHONE RANG in Mr. Pao's office at SAD headquarters in Beijing. Pao was busy examining files on politically related incidents of violence over the past five years, and he was tempted to ignore the call to avoid breaking his concentration. He grunted, put down the records and picked up the phone.

"Shi," he spoke into the phone. "How may I help you?"

"Pao?" Trent's voice inquired. "This is Carson."

"Carson," Pao remarked with a sigh. "Are you and Johnson all right? Did something happen in Shanghai, or are you just checking in?"

"We're trying to negotiate a deal with the head of a local branch of an international tong society," Trent explained.

"Tong?" Pao was stunned. "They're gangsters."

"I'm aware of that," Trent assured him, "but desperate situations can require drastic methods. I'm sure you realize sometimes one must pay the devils if one wants to ride the dragon."

"Spare me the parables, Mr. Carson," Pao snapped. "What are you doing with the tong, and what sort of deal are you talking about?"

"Please, let me explain," Trent began. "We know little about the terrorists except they are well organized, well armed, trained to some degree at least, and apparently there are a fair number of them. This suggests they must have some form of financing. Your government isn't financing them, my country isn't financing them, and apparently the Soviets aren't doing it, either. That means they're either getting backing from some nation or organization we failed to consider, or they're getting the money through sources of their own. Probably an illegal source.''

"You think the tong are responsible for the terrorism?'' Pao asked, obviously considering the notion absurd. "The tong are criminals. They aren't political.''

"Oh, the tong societies started out as political movements,'' Trent corrected. "Just as the White Lotus Society and the Yellow Turbans started as resistance movements against the Mongol and Manchu domination of China centuries ago. The slogan of the tong and Triad societies was 'overthrow the Ching and restore the Ming.' The Ching Dynasty was under Manchu rulers—''

"And the Ming Dynasty had been under Chinese rulers governing China,'' Pao said with annoyance. "I really don't need a history lesson about my own country, Mr. Carson. What do the tong have to gain by murdering tourists or Chinese civilians? I thought their interests were in profits rather than politics these days.''

"Quite true,'' Trent confirmed. "The majority of tong societies are probably glad that China has gone through these recent reforms. There are fewer restrictions now than when Mao was alive. One of the prices of a freer society is that criminals can act more freely as well. However the tong source I've contacted tells me he knows of another society, the Red Fist Tong, which is rumored to be connected with a mysterious militant Maoist organization.''

"Maoists?'' Pao seemed surprised. "I haven't heard that term for a while. Incredible, considering that just twelve years ago everyone in China claimed to be a Maoist.''

"Twelve years ago it was not healthy to claim to be anything else," Trent commented. "At any rate, the Red Fist Tong may be connected with the terrorists. They're largely involved in the opium trade. Supposedly they have contacts with Golden Triangle Triad in Southeast Asia and sell heroin to Chinese in your country, as well as exporting it to Taiwan, Australia, New Zealand, Korea, possibly even European countries."

"Sounds like a disgusting lot that deserve to be burned out of existence," Pao remarked. "May all the gods defecate on such motherless trash."

"I don't know what the gods might do with their bowels," Trent replied, "but we can do something about the Red Fist Tong and their opium business and hopefully find a lead to the terrorists in the process. My tong contact tells me the Red Fist has been making an enormous profit by increased drug trafficking recently, but no one knows where the money is going. He believes it is being used to finance the terrorists."

"Did he tell you where to find these drug-dealing toad scum?" Pao asked eagerly.

"We have to bargain for that information," Trent explained. "The tong leader gave us this much information because he is a good Chinese who loves his country and his fellow countrymen. I think the fact that the Red Fist Tong might bring more heat on all the tong societies could have something to do with his willingness to cooperate as well, but tact and good manners are necessary when negotiating terms, especially with Asians."

"So they tell me," Pao said dryly. "I take it your tong friend won't share any more information unless we offer him something in return?"

"His patriotism has a price," Trent confirmed. "In order to tell us where to find the Red Fist Tong, he feels we should grant him a favor in return. He considers it a matter of face. Giving information to the authorities for free would be bad for his reputation."

"I don't even know who he is or what part of Shanghai he's located in," Pao replied. Then he sighed and added, "What does he want?"

"He asks that the police and other authorities allow all gambling activities in Shanghai to be undisturbed for the next three months," Trent explained. "No raids, no arrests, no names taken for further prosecution or harassment."

"Gambling?" Pao was surprised. "Nothing about smuggling, prostitution, drugs or anything else? Just gambling?"

"That's right," Trent said. "The tong leader realizes that to ask more would be asking the authorities to lose face. He feels this is a reasonable request under the circumstances. Besides, he says gambling is a passion with the Chinese. Three month's profits of uninterrupted *fan-tan* will be better than six months of smuggling merchandise in and out of the country. No opium or guns involved. No harm to anyone except those who choose to throw their money away."

"All right," Pao told him. "I'll arrange it. This is China, after all. Trading and bargains are conducted on all levels. Tell your tong contact Shanghai will have undisturbed gambling for the next three months. I trust he will keep his word in return."

"I'd say we have a deal, Mr. Pao," Trent assured him.

"Hen hau," Pao replied. "Very good. You and Mr. Johnson have done very good work as well. I just hope this doesn't turn to be another false lead."

"We'll just have to find out," Trent answered. "See you in Beijing."

12

Fog drifted across the harbor. It was located near Shantou along the coast of the South China Sea, almost equidistant from Taiwan and Hong Kong. Small and obscure, the harbor was largely ignored because it was surrounded by larger and busier ports. This was ideal for the Red Fist Tong, which did business with an exclusive and clandestine clientele.

Gary Manning observed the harbor through the Starlite nightscope attached to his FAL assault rifle. The light density system of the Starlite was better than infrared because it magnified reflected light instead of emitting and receiving infrared electromagnetic waves to detect color spectrum just beyond red portion radiation. The Starlite system allowed the viewer to see more details without the possibility of temporary blindness in case of a sudden flash of bright light, which can occur with infrared telescopes.

Several figures were active on the docks. Men carried crates down a gangplank to a fishing vessel. They took the cargo to a warehouse in the center of the pier. Two trucks, deuce-and-a-half vehicles, were parked in front of the building. Other men were loading more boxes into the trucks. None of that seemed terribly suspicious, aside from the fact the harbor was supposed to be the base for the Red Fist Tong.

"I've counted twelve men down there so far," Manning whispered to his companions. "But there could be two or three times that many. Hard to say what numbers might be inside the building or on board the boat.''

Yakov Katzenelenbogen, Mr. Pao and Major Hsing were next to Manning, huddled around a bamboo fence on a grassy knoll above the harbor. The Canadian was screened by a bushy cluster of shrubbery. A space between the branches let him use the night scope without exposing himself to the men at the pier.

''Any weapons?'' Pao asked. ''Any evidence they might be unloading heroin or opium? Anything at all to suggest this isn't a legal business?''

''Not from what I can see,'' Manning was forced to admit.

''I doubt that they'd have labels on the crates to declare they had illegal narcotics inside,'' Katz commented. ''As for weapons, we'd better assume they've got them whether we can see any or not.''

''Hold on, Gray,'' Pao replied. ''So far all we have is a claim by a tong criminal leader who told your friend Carson that a fellow named Feng Teh supposedly runs the Red Fist Tong dope-smuggling operations through that harbor. That's hardly ample proof to justify swooping down on them like killer hawks.''

''You said we had enough grounds to raid them,'' Katz insisted. The Israeli, like the others, had donned black camouflage uniform and boots. A Uzi submachine gun hung from a shoulder strap by his left hip and the SIG-Sauer autoloader was holstered under his right arm. The belt around his waist contained several spare magazine pouches, some grenades and a two-way radio.

''This is one hell of a time to debate whether or not to take action,'' Manning remarked. ''We're here, dammit. I thought we had a plan.''

"We're still going through with the plan," Pao assured him. "But we can't run down there and start shooting. I told you that before."

"Vargas and Johnson are in position," Katz declared. "I'll signal them as soon as we're ready to go. Major, you'd better join your men and make sure they understand what to do. No last minute foul-ups."

"Our role is simple," Hsing answered. "You and your people will be taking the bulk of the risk."

"That's the way we work," Katz explained. "Besides, we need to take some prisoners, and we want to save as much evidence as possible. Evidence of the Red Fist Tong's illegal drug trade and, more important, any evidence that might lead to the terrorists. I'm sure your troops are very good, Major, but they're relatively inexperienced. If a firefight occurs, we don't want them endangering their lives or anybody else's if it isn't necessary. More to the point, in the heat of battle, they'll be inclined to shoot anyone who comes at them and even lob grenades. We don't want to have a massacre or destroy whatever might be inside that building."

"We don't want that, either," Pao assured him. "Where did you assign Mr. Carson? The fellow who likes to lecture on Asian history?"

"He and Masters are together," Katz answered.

"Good," Pao remarked. "They deserve each other."

"Just let my men get into position before you do anything," Katz urged. "Otherwise, we might have a slaughter on our hands, and it won't be the tong who gets the ax."

David McCarter and John Trent moved silently among the shadows surrounding the warehouse. The art of stealthfully approaching an enemy stronghold required infinite care and patience. Slowly moving from cover to cover, trying to blend into the surroundings and avoiding sudden movements, was a stressful, nerve-racking task.

Under ordinary conditions, McCarter tended to be impatient, fidgety and short-tempered, but the battlefield was his natural state. He had the patience of Job as he crept toward the harbor. McCarter concentrated on moving silently, keeping to the shadows and making the most of the sparse cover. The familiar rush of blood in his veins already began as the tension mounted. McCarter loved the excitement of his job. Risking one's life was the ultimate gamble, and the British ace had long ago realized he was addicted to the sensations and thrills of his profession. He suspected psychologists would say there was something mentally wrong with him. McCarter did not know if they might not be at least partly right, but he didn't worry about it.

McCarter figured people like that had learned about human behavior in a classroom. They gained their understanding of people from books, written by individuals who probably knew less about what makes people tick than the average fellow, who learns simply by living. Maybe if a shrink had experienced the excitement of combat, felt the adrenaline pump through his veins as the senses sharpened to their full potential, the mind clear-cutting as a well-honed razor because one is at the ultimate level of being alive when the possibility of sudden death is closest— maybe then McCarter would consider the fellow's opinion of him worth listening to. In the meantime, those psychologists did not know what the hell they were talking about, as far as McCarter was concerned.

The British commando was clad in black camies and rubber-soled boots, with a black beret pulled over his head. He carried a KG-99 machine pistol by a shoulder strap, a nine-inch silencer attached to the barrel. McCarter's pet 9 mm Browning pistol was holstered under his left arm, and he carried spare magazines, two fragmentation M-26 grenades and two SAS "flash-bang" concussion grenades. The

Briton was ready for action and eager to do what he did best, which was also what he privately believed he had been born to do.

John Trent was also dressed in black, the traditional night garments of a ninja. His head was covered by a wrapped cloth hood and a scarf-mask that covered his face except for the eyes. The *gi*-style jacket and pants contained numerous pockets with weapons hidden inside. A black shoulder holster rig held a Ruger P-85 pistol under his left arm and the *ninja-do* sword was thrust in a black sash around his waist. Split-toe *tabi* boots covered his feet, and a single-edge, razor-sharp knife was strapped to his ankle. The knife was balanced for throwing, and the sheath and handle were black.

Trained in *ninjutsu* since childhood, Trent was an expert in stealth and camouflage. He silently followed McCarter, blending into the shadows with skill equal to the Briton's. Perhaps even better, McCarter thought with admiration for the ninja's ability. They advanced to the storage shed at the edge of the pier. A stocky, well-muscled sentry stood near the shed. The collar of his coat was turned up to protect him from the chilly fog-laced breeze, but the coat was unbuttoned. McCarter noticed the stubby barrel of a compact, box-shaped metal object peeking out from under the coat.

McCarter recognized the object. It was a Ingram MAC-10 machine pistol. The Briton had carried a MAC-10 into combat on numerous missions. Until he recently switched to the KG-99, the Ingram had been his standard weapon. An ass-kicking little room-cleaner, the MAC-10 used a 32-round magazine and fired the projectiles at close to a thousand rounds per minute. Another interesting fact about the Ingram occurred to McCarter. The gun was manufactured in the United States.

The terrorist strike against Chinese civilians had been carried out with men armed with American-made weapons, the Briton recalled. The excitement was building a fire in his stomach. These must be the right bunch of bastards, McCarter thought, gripping his KG-99.

The sentry's attention was turned toward the grassy knoll approximately one kilometer from the harbor. He must have seen or heard something along the bamboo fence where most of the raid unit was located. Another sentry had also taken an interest in the knoll, but the fog cover made it difficult for them to be sure what they were seeing.

"Ting zhi!" Pao's voice bellowed through a bullhorn. "Stop! All persons at the harbor, stop immediately and put your hands overhead! This is the Social Affairs Department! You are ordered to step onto the pier in plain view, hands raised and offer no resistance."

The dockworkers immediately threw down their crates and dashed in all directions. Many headed for the warehouse, while others ran to the gangplank of the fishing boat or ducked behind the cover of stacked crates already on the pier. Most reached inside their jackets for handguns, but some were only armed with sheath knives on their belts.

The sentry drew his Ingram machine pistol and opened fire in the direction of the bamboo fence. The flame from the muzzle cast a harsh glare across the pier as the weapon roared with full-auto fury and spent cartridge casings spewed from the ejector port. He was too preoccupied with the task to notice David McCarter slip from the shadows behind him. The Briton quickly stepped closer and hammered the butt of his KG-99 between the sentry's shoulder blades.

The thug groaned and collapsed unconscious on the wooden walkway. Two dockworkers saw McCarter slug the sentry. They swung their pistols toward the Briton. A metal object whistled from the shadows and struck one of the gunmen in the side of the head. The sharp steel points of the *shaken* throwing star pierced flesh and bit into the man's skull. Shrieking in agony, he dropped his pistol and clasped both hands to his head as he fell to his knees. He tried to pull the *shaken* from his skull, but the effort to dislodge the tines forced one point into the temple. It punctured bone and stabbed the brain within. He flopped on his back, twitched violently and then lay still as death itself.

The second gunman was startled when his comrade screamed. He just had time to note the ghastly steel tumor attached to his companion's head. McCarter took advantage of the gunman's distraction and snap-aimed with the KG-99, triggering a three-round burst. The 9 mm parabellum slugs smashed into the pistol-packer's chest, slicing into the left lung and bursting the heart. The man hurtled backward and fell heavily beside his slain companion. His wounded heart bled what little remained of his life in a matter of microseconds.

McCarter ran for shelter behind a stack of crates as two more thugs turned their attention toward him. He heard angry voices shout something in Chinese, accompanied by pistol shots. McCarter ducked around the crates as bullets splintered wood from the boxes. Fragments showered the Briton's bowed head and shoulders like toothpick dandruff.

"Tsang-bai zhu!" screamed the tong enforcer who was already concealed behind the crates.

"Oh, God!" McCarter hissed through clenched teeth as he raised the KG-99 to ward off the flashing blade in the other man's fist.

The thug swung the knife at McCarter, but the six-inch curved blade struck the steel frame of the machine pistol. McCarter's free hand slashed a hard karate chop across his opponent's wrist to prevent another attack. The knife dropped from inert fingers, but the man's other hand quickly seized McCarter's wrist above the KG-99 to shove the weapon upward at the sky.

McCarter whipped a knee for his opponent's groin. The other man attempted the same tactic, and their knees crashed painfully together. Both men grunted as bone met bone. McCarter swiftly executed his favorite close-quarters street-fighting move, one he learned as a kid in the East End of London. He snapped his head forward and butted his opponent in the face. The frontal bone caught the Asian between the eyes. McCarter heard him yelp with pain and surprise. He grabbed the man's shirtfront with his left hand and yanked him forward to receive a second head butt, even harder than the first.

The Asian started to sag. His grip on McCarter's right wrist loosened. The Briton rammed a knee to the man's abdomen and swiftly grabbed him by the neck to thwart a response. A final shove of the opponent's head against the crates, making it rap the merciless wood hard, and the matter was decided in favor of the British ace.

The two gunmen who had opened fire on McCarter charged toward the pile of crates, pistols in hand. One glanced down at the bodies of their slain comrades. He was surprised and puzzled by the steel star lodged in the skull of one corpse. The Asian failed to understand that until John Trent suddenly materialized from the shadows.

The ninja's sword hissed from its scabbard as Trent jumped beside the startled gunmen. The sword rose overhead to meet his other hand and swiftly descended in a *shomin-uch* stroke. The razor-sharp steel struck one Chinese killer as he started to turn his head. The blade divided his face from hairline to upper lip. The man was dead before he could fire his pistol.

The second gunman fired a hasty shot with his T-51 autoloader. Trent had already stepped forward and pivoted on his right foot, arm extended, sword in his fist like the blade of a sickle. The 7.65 mm bullet buzzed inches from Trent's head as his body kept moving. The force of the motion slashed the sword across the chest of the tong triggerman. Blood splashed the Asian hoodlum's shirt-front as the deep gash opened up.

He cried out and fired the pistol again, but he had staggered backward, and his shot went wild, tearing a useless hole in the fog. Trent completed his pivot and swung the sword in a fast diagonal cut. It sliced through the side of the gunman's neck, severed vertebrae and chopped off his head with a single blow. The severed skull hit the ground and rolled eight feet before it came to a halt. The features displayed utter astonishment. The eyes blinked once and stayed open to stare into the realm of the dead forever.

Another Red Fist stooge gasped in horror as he saw the grisly decapitated corpse of one of his comrades sink to the ground. A figure dressed in black, like a ninja of ancient Japan, stood over the body with a bloodstained sword in his fists. It seemed impossible, yet the figure was real. The amazed and angry hoodlum raised his Hong Kong import .38 revolver and aimed.

A 7.62 mm rifle slug smashed into his skull behind the right ear. The man felt a brief instant of incredible pain and then plunged into the oblivion of death. Gary Manning had spotted the man as he approached the pier. The Canadian marksman quickly aimed his FAL rifle, located the head in the cross hairs of the Starlite scope and took him out with a single bullet.

Manning headed for the trucks while other members of the raid unit fired at the tong enforcers on the pier and inside the warehouse. The Canadian guessed that some of the enemy would use the trucks for cover and possibly try to destroy the contents of the crates already loaded into the vehicles. He saw two pairs of legs at the opposite side of the closest truck as he approached. Part of his theory was certainly right.

He switched the FAL to full-auto mode as he peered under the truck. Manning pointed the rifle at the limbs and fired a controlled spray of six rounds. Shrieks responded to the tactic and the two thugs collapsed, clawing at their bullet-smashed shins and kneecaps.

Another man appeared at the rear of the rig, a Type 50 submachine gun in his fists. Manning swung his FAL toward the gunman, braced the butt stock against a hip and fired a trio of 7.62 mm slugs directly into the center of the thug's narrow chest. The impact pitched the man backward, making him trigger his Chinese chopper and blast a harmless salvo overhead.

Movement at the front of the vehicle drew Manning's attention, and he whirled to fire another three-round burst at somebody who had stuck his arm out the window of the cab with a pistol in the fist. Two bullets sang harshly against the metal door and whined in protest. The third chopped through the gunman's forearm. The pistol hopped out of his hand and the Red Fist flunky retreated inside the cab. His howls of agony revealed that the bullet had not merely creased the hoodlum.

Manning dashed to the cab and jumped onto the running board by the door. The astonished man behind the wheel stared at him with disbelief and terror, clutching his wounded arm with his other hand. Manning raised the FAL and reversed the grip in a single swift action. He thrust the butt stock through the open window for a decisive knockout tap on the head.

The Phoenix commando hopped down from the cab and headed toward the end of the vehicle, just in time to see a figure leap from the back of the deuce-and-a-half and burst into a desperate run for the warehouse. Manning was one of the top demolition men in the world. He instantly guessed the man had bailed out to try to save his ass from being blown to bits.

The Canadian instinctively dived to the ground and covered his head with one arm. He realized that any explosion powerful enough to destroy the truck would certainly kill as well, but there was no time to run for cover elsewhere and no place to run to except the other truck or the warehouse full of Red Fist Tong. He lay on his belly and peered under the truck. One of the men he had shot in the lower legs had passed out from the pain and shock. The other lay on his back and stared back at Manning. His features were twisted with agony and rage, his dark eyes were still determined to fight back. The guy had a T-51 autoloader in his fist and he raised the pistol from the ground to point it at Manning.

The explosion erupted inside the truck, a loud bang followed by a dragon roar of sudden flames, which swiftly rose to set the canvas roof ablaze. The man had set some sort of pyro charge, thermite or something similar, before he jumped from the rig. The fire instantly set the cargo inside the truck aflame and the canvas soon became a burning shroud over the hull of the charred wood ribs of the vehicle.

Manning was accustomed to explosions. He had been using demolitions since he was a kid working at his uncle's engineering sites in Ontario and Alberta. He barely flinched when the truck went up, but the wounded gunman was naturally alarmed and frightened by the blast. The Chinese hood forgot about Manning and covered his face with his arms.

The demolition pro realized if the charge had been powerful enough to blow up the truck it would have already exploded and he would have been torn apart by the blast. Yet there was still considerable danger because the fuel tank could blow when the fire reached the cab, and the cargo might include combustible materials. These thoughts raced through Manning's mind as he slithered under the vehicle and pointed the FAL at the thug who had threatened him with the pistol.

The man uncovered his face to see Manning crawling toward him. He hissed something in Chinese and tried to aim his T-51 at the Canadian. The Phoenix pro's rifle snarled a trio of flesh-shredders into the man's face. The thug's skull came apart like an eggshell. Brains and blood formed a gory pool around the dead man's head as Manning crawled to the opposite side of the truck.

Manning tried to avoid looking at the corpse as he crawled out from under the vehicle. He had seen enough mutilated human remains in the past and had no desire to examine this one. Manning rose and scrambled to the next truck as the flames continued to consume the first vehicle.

A man stepped down from the rear of the truck, a crate held braced to his shoulder. He saw Manning and immediately hurled the box at the Canadian. Manning ducked and raised his FAL to protect his head. The crate struck the rifle hard and knocked it from Manning's hands. The box hit the ground, and the wood cracked to leak white powder.

The tong goon shouted a martial arts battle cry and charged. He snap-kicked Manning in the belly. The Canadian folded with a grunt, but managed to clasp his hands together and swing his arms in a fast cross-body stroke. The doubled fists chopped the tong hood across the jaw and sent him staggering back to the rear of the second truck. Manning did not give his opponent a chance to recover. He dashed forward and let loose with a hard uppercut to the stomach.

The man doubled up with a groan and Manning chopped the side of his other hand across the thug's neck. The Phoenix fighter slammed a knee under the guy's jaw and the man dropped senseless to the ground. Sudden movement from the opening of the truck warned Manning of another attacker. He turned to see a knife blade swing toward his face like the Grim Reaper's scythe.

Manning weaved his head away from the sharp steel. The blade flashed less than an inch from the tip of his nose. He glimpsed the attacker, poised at the tailgate of the truck, knife raised in his fist. The flames of the burning vehicle illuminated the assassin's Asian features. The face was wild and desperate, like that of a cornered animal. Manning knew how the man felt. Nearly getting a facial with a knife blade hadn't filled him with a sense of well-being, either.

The Canadian's hand streaked out and seized the forearm above the knife blade. With his other hand he grabbed the guy's shirtfront. He pulled hard, stepped backward and turned to increase the force of his pull. The hoodlum cried out with surprise and fear as he was yanked out of the back of the truck. He sailed head over heels and crash-landed on his back.

Manning stepped forward and stomped his right boot heel onto the fist around the knife handle. Bone popped and the dazed thug howled as his fingers were broken. Manning folded his left leg and dropped forward to slam the knee in the man's midsection. He heard a breathless moan, followed by the sickly gurgle as the man began to vomit. Manning knelt on his opponent's belly, and one more blow of his fist turned the gurgle to a wheezing, choking sound. Manning felt the man's body convulse beneath him for a moment and then go limp and unconscious.

FENG TEH AND THE OTHER MEN aboard the fishing boat saw the battle erupt across the harbor. They also saw that their forces were getting chewed up by the other side. Army riflemen kept their distance and picked off sentries and bogus dockworkers with well-placed shots. Only a few raiders closed in to take on opponents at close quarters, but they were extraordinary fighting men. Feng's tong enforcers were no match for the commandos. They handled their weapons like demons commanded by the gods of war.

Bodies were strewn across the pier, bodies of dead Red Fist Tong. One of the trucks had burst into flames and burned until it ignited the gas tank. The vehicle exploded and splashed the other truck with the fuel. The second rig burned while the remaining tong forces tried to defend the harbor from the warehouse or the cover of stacks of crates on the pier.

Feng cursed as he hurried along the port side to enter the cabin deck. The tong leader yanked open a cabinet and checked the weapons stored inside. Most of the arsenal had already been claimed by other men on the boat. Feng chose an Italian-made M-12 submachine gun and stomped up the stairs to the bridge. Captain Chung was crouched by a window in the wheelhouse, an old British Webley VI revolver in his fist.

"Chung!" Feng exclaimed. "Get us out of here!"

"There will be patrols waiting for us at sea," Chung replied. He was afraid to raise his head because shots pelted the side of the boat as the harbor firefight continued. "They said they are SAD. The government and the military are involved, Feng Teh. Patrol boats are certainly already in position to cut us off if we try to flee."

"If we head north," Feng agreed, "but we will travel toward Taiwan or Hong Kong. They will not follow us outside of Chinese waters."

"The patrols will open fire on us," Chung insisted. "They don't have to catch up with us. They just have to get within range. Besides, they can radio the Taiwanese or the authorities in Hong Kong to have us seized as soon as we reach their waters."

"They won't hold us without evidence," Feng insisted. "Just get us out of here. When we get clear of the port, we throw everything overboard which could connect us with any illegal activities. Opium, heroin, guns, the whole lot. If there is no evidence, they'll let us go. Believe me, Chung. I've been in similar situations before. The Red Fist Tong has connections in Taiwan and Hong Kong. Lawyers, regional politicians, police officials and others. We'll be fine if we can get away from this spot."

"How do we explain the bullet holes?" Chung demanded.

"Let me worry about that," Feng told him. "Just start the engines."

Chung waddled to the controls, still afraid to raise his head. He switched on the motor and pulled the throttle. The engine growled and chugged within the vessel. But the boat did not move. Captain Chung checked the instruments.

"Something is wrong," he announced grimly.

"What?" Feng demanded. "What can it be?"

"I don't know—" Chung began, but his eyes widened as the probable cause dawned on him. "The propeller!"

Captain Chung was right, although he had failed to guess the exact source. Rafael Encizo and Calvin James had swum underwater to the stern of the boat. The veteran Cuban frogman had once taught scuba diving for a living in Florida, and James was a former SEAL commando for the U.S. Navy in Vietnam. The pair were superb frogmen. When the shooting started, they placed a small limpet mine on the propeller. The explosion was not very dramatic, hardly noticed by the men on board the boat, who naturally assumed the convulsions aft were caused by the bullets slamming into the vessel.

The explosion had torn loose the propeller. James and Encizo climbed up the starboard side, aware the crew would be preoccupied with the firefight on the port side. They hauled themselves over the handrail, water dripping from their black wet suits. Encizo pushed back the diving mask onto his forehead with one hand and gripped a spear gun in the other. He gazed about the decks and saw no sign of anyone starboard.

James pulled a large waterproof rubber bag from the water by a strong nylon cord. He placed it on the deck and drew the USN combat knife from the sheath on his ankle. The molded black handle offered a sure grip underwater as well as out. James used the six-inch parkerized blade to cut open the bag. Encizo unbuckled the harness to his air tank and removed his diving fins.

"So far, so good," James whispered as he removed from the bag a Type 50 submachine gun with a twelve-inch silencer attached to the barrel, and an H&K MP-5 machine pistol, also with silencer.

"It's not over yet," Encizo replied, checking his Seiko diver's watch. They were right on time. Everything seemed to be going according to schedule.

James handed him the Heckler and Koch subgun. Encizo reached into the bag and located a utility belt with a holster containing his H&K P-9S autoloader, and ammo pouches with magazines for the MP-5 and the pistol. James removed his scuba gear and took another belt from the bag with his Beretta 92-F in hip holster and ammo pouches attached. Both men buckled on the belts and loaded full magazines into the submachine guns.

Encizo fished inside the bag to get a concussion grenade and a small flare gun. He attached the former to his belt and inserted the latter inside his wet suit. The Cuban drew his P-9S from the hip holster and worked the slide to jack a round in the chamber. Encizo liked Heckler & Koch firearms. The P-9S was a well-made, sturdy double-action 9 mm pistol with a nine-round magazine. He switched on the safety catch and returned the H&K side arm to the holster.

James virtually repeated Encizo's actions with his own gear. He was less than thrilled with the Chinese T-50 subgun. Not that he had any complaint about the weapon design or firepower. He had used the T-50 and its Soviet counterpart a few times in the past and found the subguns performed well enough. James simply wished he had a more familiar weapon. The M-16 rifle he had brought from the States was too long to use effectively in extreme close-quarters combat such as inside the small compartments of the fishing vessel. The T-50 with its folding stock and ten-and-a-half-inch barrel was better suited for the task.

At least the Beretta on his hip was a well-known piece, loaded with a fifteen-round magazine. A small medic kit was attached to the belt at the small of his back. Equipment to save life as well as take it. James nodded to Encizo. The Cuban returned the gesture. They were ready to take the boat.

A figure appeared at the stern. The tong smuggler gasped with surprise when he spotted the muscular Hispanic and the tall black man. He carried a Taiwan-made T-36 submachine gun, a weapon modeled more or less on the design of the old U.S. M-3A1 "grease gun." The thug pointed the .45-caliber chopper at the Phoenix pair.

Encizo triggered the spear gun at virtually the same moment as James fired his T-50. The silenced Chinese subgun rasped harshly and spat out three 7.62 mm slugs while the harpoon hissed from the Cuban's unorthodox weapon, propelled by a powerful CO_2 cartridge. The trio of bullets ripped a line of holes in the gunman's chest from solar plexus to the hollow of his throat. The harpoon struck to the left of the breastbone and pierced the hoodlum's heart. He fell backward to the deck, the T-36 unfired in his hands.

An alarmed voice cried out something from the stern, and James and Encizo did not need to understand Chinese to know someone had seen the corpse of the smuggler fall. The black warrior promptly took the concussion grenade from his belt, pulled the pin and lobbed it at the stern. His aim was flawless. The grenade hit the starboard quarter, bounced and hurled toward the port quarter.

Startled voices echoed from the stern. The smugglers were trying to catch the elusive, bouncing grenade. They did not have long to try. The concussion blast erupted with fury that violently rocked the trawler. A man hurtled overboard and splashed in the cold water beyond. Several voices cried out in pain.

James rushed to the stern and swung around the edge of the cabin bulkhead. He found four Red Tong enthusiasts sprawled across the deck. Three were unconscious and another groaned as he clasped his hands over his head. His eardrums had been shattered. A fifth opponent was on his knees, one hand braced against some crates while the other pressed the side of his skull as blood seeped from his left ear. Yet another Chinese thug rose unsteadily to his feet, a Type 56 rifle clutched in his hands.

The man was dazed, and blood trickled from his nostrils. The concussion blast had put most of the enemy out of commission, but unfortunately, the fellow was still armed and potentially dangerous. James had no choice. He triggered his T-50 and shot the man.

James turned toward the stunned hood who seemed in slightly better shape than his comrades. He raised the subgun to smack the man behind the ear. Suddenly the thug swung away from the crate and lashed out with a stevedore hook in his fist.

The big steel claw caught the frame of James's T-50 chopper. A boot slammed into the black warrior's midsection and kicked breath from his lungs. A hard yank wrenched the subgun from James's grasp. The weapon clattered to the deck as the thug swung a roundhouse swipe with the hook.

James weaved away, and the sharp point narrowly missed his face. Swiftly swinging a backhand sweep with the hook, the Chinese tried to smash James's skull with the curved portion of the steel hook. The American warrior ducked beneath the murderous swing, the weapon whirled above his head, and he slapped his hands to the deck and kicked out with both legs.

He trapped the killer's calves between his legs in a scissors hold. James rolled his body and yanked the man's feet out from under him. The tong flunky cried out with surprise and fell to the deck. James released the scissors grip and slithered away as his opponent swung the hook at the Phoenix pro's legs. Again, the criminal's weapon missed its target. As the point struck the wooden deck, the sharp steel bit deep in the wooden surface. The tong enforcer yanked hard to try to dislodge the weapon.

James rolled on his side and thrust out a bare foot. The heel smashed into the Asian's face, breaking the bridge of his nose on impact. Stunned by the kick, the thug fell backward. James scrambled forward and pounced on his opponent. He pinned down the forearm above the fist with the hook and punched the man in the face. His hand rose and chopped his opponent across the side of the neck. The body under him went limp. James reached for the USN sheath knife, but realized his opponent was out cold, so he left the knife in its sheath and rose to retrieve his T-50 subgun.

ENCIZO HAD BEEN ATTACKED by two tong killers charging from the bow of the fishing vessel. He dropped to one knee and fired a volley of 9 mm rounds into the pair. One man spun about from the force of the two H&K slugs in the chest. He hit the handrail and toppled over the side to plunge into the sea. The other thug doubled up with three bullets in his stomach and upper intestines. Encizo nailed him with another burst of MP-5 missiles that drilled into the man's head.

A hastily dispatched shot barked from the window of the bridge above Encizo. The big .455 bullet split a deck plank near Encizo's right knee. Instantly the Cuban responded by raising his MP-5 and blasting a stream of rounds at the would-be assassin, the window shattering from the fury of high-velocity projectiles. Although the gunman retreated from the window, Encizo was not sure if he hit the trigger-man or not.

The Cuban jumped to his feet and dashed to the bow. He swung the barrel of the MP-5 around the corner of the cabin trunk and fired a fast salvo to discourage any possible opponents from launching an attack. Encizo whirled around the corner to discover one man sprawled on the deck, his upper torso riddled with bullet holes. Another was huddled near the handrail. He glanced up fearfully at Encizo and raised his hands in surrender. Encizo did not have time to take a prisoner—not when there were still more opponents to deal with.

"Jump in the water!" Encizo ordered.

The man looked at him in fear but without comprehension. Encizo thought about repeating the order in Spanish, but decided that would not get any more success than English. He resorted to a different method to express his desires. The Cuban fired a three-round burst near the man's feet. Bullets ripped into the deck next to the hoodlum, and he instinctively grabbed the handrail and vaulted over it to leap into the water. A loud splash followed him.

Another burst of automatic fire snarled from above, and bullets raked the bow near Encizo's position. The Cuban heard the tinkling sound of shattering glass mixed with the chattering report of the full-auto weapon. He dived for the corner of the cabin trunk at port side as bullets chewed at the deck. Another attack from the bridge, Encizo thought. This time with a submachine gun instead of a pistol. Either the opponent at the bridge had a choice of weapons, or there was more than one man up there.

The tong forces port side had suffered numerous losses from the combatants on the pier. Several corpses already littered the deck. Calvin James had also opened fire from the stern, forcing the two survivors to bolt for the bow. Encizo cut off their escape from the bow and blasted them with his MP-5. They tumbled lifeless to the deck.

James waved his weapon and signaled to Encizo that he knew he was there and would hold his fire. The Cuban moved to the entrance of the cabin deck below the bridge, swapping magazines to reload his MP-5 as he approached the threshold. An explosion on the pier startled him, and he glanced at the harbor as a stack of crates burst into kindling and was flung skyward along with the mangled corpses of two more of the Red Fist Tong. The pair had been using the crates for cover, and one of the raiders had taken them out with a well-tossed grenade.

The battle on the harbor itself was virtually over. Katz, Manning and Pao commanded one group of soldiers who steadily drove the tong followers into the warehouse from the front, while McCarter, Trent, Major Hsing and a few other Chinese troopers herded them inside the building from the rear. Boxed into the warehouse, the raiders would then lob in tear gas grenades to subdue the surviving enemies. If there were still those who tried to resist, concussion grenades would be thrown in as well to knock the fight out of them before the Phoenix Force commandos and their allies entered the building.

Not a bad idea, Encizo thought, taking the concussion grenade from his belt.

He glanced up at the bridge and noticed a ladder by the port side that extended to the top deck. Encizo raised his H&K chattergun and sprayed a volley of 9 mm rounds at the bridge to discourage any assaults from that direction. Glass smashed as bullets shattered windowpanes. Encizo pulled the pin from the grenade and tossed the blaster into the cabin deck. James saw the Cuban throw the grenade and steeled himself for the concussion blast.

The entire boat trembled from the violent shock of the explosion. Encizo pointed at James and then indicated the cabin threshold to signal for his partner to go in to check on opponents who might lurk in the cabin deck. Anyone in there would not present much of a threat, not after the effects of a concussion grenade in such a small enclosure.

Encizo grabbed the rungs to the ladder and climbed to the bridge, the barrel of the MP-5 leading the way. He reached the top and moved to a window whose glass had been blown away by projectiles during the battle. Encizo carefully peered inside to find Feng Teh and Captain Chung on the floor within.

Both men had been thrown off balance when the grenade exploded. Chung had caught a bullet in his right shoulder and was trying to cradle his arm to his chest without releasing the Webley revolver in his left fist. Feng had received a deep gash under the right eye from flying glass, but he still held on to the Beretta M-12. Encizo guessed Feng must be important or would not be in the bridge with the captain. The Cuban did not want to kill someone who promised to be a useful source of information.

Encizo held the MP-5 in one fist and drew the P-9S pistol from the holster on his hip. Then he swung around to face the window, his submachine gun pointed at Feng and the H&K autoloader aimed at Chung. He elevated the P-9S slightly and fired a single round into the control by the wheel. The bullet whined against metal and ricocheted into the ceiling. The warning shot startled the two Chinese gangsters. They glanced up. Each man stared into the muzzle of a weapon.

"Give it up or die," Encizo announced. "I don't know if you understand what I'm saying, but you'd better get the idea fast. Either of you move, you're both dead."

"No!" Chung declared, tossing his Webley aside and holding his left hand high. Blood stained the palm. "I surrender."

Feng glared at Encizo. He gripped the Beretta subgun tighter, but did not raise the weapon. Life or death. The choice was clear. Death did not appeal to him, but neither did prison. He would probably be executed for his crimes anyway—unless he could make a deal with his captors. After all, this was China.

"We need talk," Feng declared, shoving the M-12 across the floor. "Talk about deal. Yes?"

"Don't count on it, fella," Encizo replied with a shrug.

13

"We certainly captured a talkative little bastard," Mr. Pao announced as he entered the conference room, accompanied by Calvin James and Yakov Katzenelenbogen. "Feng Teh is eager and willing to sell out his comrades. So much for honor among thieves."

"Terrorists and drug smugglers make thieves seem downright charming by comparison," Gary Manning commented, helping himself to a cup of black Indonesian coffee. "So what did Feng have to say?"

"He claims he's working with a terrorist group called the People's New Guard," Pao explained, taking a seat at the head of the table. "The leader is supposedly a woman named Kuo Chun. We pulled her record from our files on political activists. It is a very old record, but fascinating nonetheless."

"What sort of political activist are we talking about here?" David McCarter asked. The Briton sat at the table with his KG-99 disassembled in front of him. He carefully cleaned the parts with gun oil and a rag, occasionally puffing on a Player's cigarette. "Left-wing, right-wing or somewhere in the middle?"

"As Albert Pauphilet once said," Katz remarked, taking a seat next to Pao, "no mind is so like the extreme right as the extreme left."

"Well, we are certainly talking about the extreme left in Kuo Chun's case," Pao confirmed. He placed a file folder on the table as he spoke. "She was born in 1948, here in Beijing. Parents were members of the Communist Party and devout supporters of Chairman Mao. Regional cell leaders in the 1950s and early sixties. Their daughter was naturally raised to be a good Communist, and in those days that meant you did whatever Chairman Mao wanted. She became a member of Mao's youth movement, the Red Guard."

"This is beginning to sound a bit familiar," Encizo commented. "We came across a couple ex-Red Guard fanatics in Africa a few years ago. They were involved in terrorist activity there, too."

"Many of us were members of the Red Guard," Yang said defensively. "We were patriots, young party members who displayed the support of our political convictions by marching in the streets with our copies of *The Quotations of Chairman Mao* held high. We chanted and we rallied because we felt enthusiasm for Mao and what he represented. There was a great sense of national unity and strong belief in our cause."

"There was more than that involved in the Red Guard and you know it, Yang," Pao declared with a sigh. "That's a part of our history we have to accept, whether we like it or not. The whole world knows what the Red Guard did. Pretending it never happened won't make those memories go away."

Everyone in the room knew what Pao was talking about. Twenty years earlier the Red Guard had been a symbol of Mainland China. That alarmed most of the other nations of the world because the huge mobs of millions of Chinese zealots swearing their devotion to Mao and Communism were too similar to the Hitler Youth Movement in Germany. The comparison went beyond surface similarities.

The Red Guard attacked individuals of "questionable loyalty." Some of these were writers and artists who previously had been asked by the state to contribute ideas and material with their personal views concerning the Communist regime. After obeying this request, they often became victimized for the very material they had been asked to submit. Anything that even remotely criticized Mao or the Party was condemned as a form of political heresy, and the Red Guard was eager to punish the heretics.

Anyone who might express "pro-Western ideas" or "capitalistic materialism" could also be targets of Red Guard violence. Intellectuals were also victims, scholars who dared place Lao-tsu, Confucius or Plato on a level above the works of Mao. Those suspected of participating in covert religious services, usually Buddhist, Taoist or Muslim, were also regarded as enemies of the state. Homes were destroyed, people beaten, humiliated, sometimes even tortured or murdered by the Guard.

The Red Guard even lashed out at China's own history. They burned ancient literary works of distant dynasties that represented "the imperialism of the past." Works of art, priceless remnants of China's incredible heritage, were smashed and lost forever. Temples, monuments, palaces were attacked and vandalized. Wonders of one of the oldest and most magnificent cultures in the world were wiped away by the screaming, brainwashed fanatics of the Red Guard.

These extremist actions became so widespread and frequent, Mao himself tried to disband the Red Guard. Some cells were comprised of such extremists that they refused to believe the decree, certain that they were the only individuals who truly knew the will of Mao Tse-tung. A monster had been created, and even Chairman Mao could not stop it entirely.

"Let's just concentrate on Kuo Chun," Katz suggested tactfully, aware that the Chinese would probably avoid discussing the Red Guard in detail.

"Kuo was a cell leader with the Red Guard," Pao explained, consulting his records. "She was regarded as a great youth leader in the sixties. Kuo received commendations for her efforts to assemble large groups of young people. Supposedly she was a very influential speaker and led her followers by example. But she got in some trouble even then. Kuo's cell vandalized the former Imperial Palace in Beijing as an act of protest against imperialism everywhere. In fact she was arrested in 1969 for this stunt. They also attacked and injured several people in the process, including three police officers. However, since the Red Guard was still a respected institution at the time, charges were dropped, and she was simply warned about misconduct."

"Girls will be girls," Manning muttered.

"Kuo was suspected of several other 'misconducts,'" Pao continued, "but charges were always dropped or there was never any solid proof against her. Some of these actions included a number of vicious assaults and two murders. The file ends on the date of August 10, 1976, almost one month from the day Mao died. Kuo seems to have vanished. There were considerable efforts to find her. Kuo's name came up during the trial of the Gang of Four. There were claims that Kuo and a secret cell of Red Guard radicals were conspiring with Mao's widow, Jiang Qing, and the three members of the politburo that comprised the Gang of Four, in their attempts to overthrow the government and take over China."

Whether or not the charges against the Gang of Four were valid was not the indisputable fact Pao seemed to think it to be. Many still questioned whether Jiang Qing and the officials from the politburo had actually conspired to overthrow the government, or whether they were trumped-up charges in order to have an excuse to get rid of the greatest loyalists of Mao's regime. More than a million

Chinese were arrested for being part of this alleged conspiracy, and more than seven thousand were executed. Yet apparently none of the men in the room intended to argue about the Gang of Four or events connected with it.

"But Kuo was never found?" Encizo asked.

"No, she never stood trial and frankly no one has been looking for her too hard for the past ten years or so," Pao admitted. "It's believed she probably fled the country; perhaps headed for North Korea or some other place forsaken by the gods. It's possible she has been in hiding all these years, putting together whatever mad scheme she has in mind with this terrorist business."

"Feng may not be telling the truth," Yang complained. "How can we take the word of a filthy tong hoodlum?"

"He was telling the truth," James assured Yang. "We interrogated Feng with and without scopolamine and the story came out the same both times. Well, he confessed to a lot of criminal stuff under the influence of truth serum, which he wouldn't have admitted without that kind of prompting. What he's told us about Commander Kuo and the other ringleaders of the People's New Guard is the truth."

"What other leaders?" CIA agent Ross inquired, anxiously tapping a pencil on the tabletop.

"The one that interests the SAD most is Ming Ssu," Pao answered. "Ming was one of our agents back in the seventies. Very good at his job. According to our file on Ming, he was acknowledged as a expert in espionage, propaganda tactics and strategy. He also appeared to have been a rather ambitious individual. Intelligent, tough, potentially very dangerous."

"You're referring to Ming in the past tense," Encizo noticed.

"Ming Ssu has been officially dead since 1978," Pao explained. "His body, or at least *a body*, was found burned beyond recognition by what appeared to be a car accident. The car crashed into a truck transporting acid to an industrial site. The acid destroyed the face and most of the flesh of the corpse. Fire took most of the rest. The identification was made from our personnel dental records."

"If Ming was clever enough and had the right opportunities, he may have switched the dental records with the victim supplying the corpse," Manning remarked.

"Would Ming have been the sort to join forces with an outfit like the New Guard?" Ross inquired.

"Oddly enough, that isn't in his file," Pao said sarcastically. "All we know for certain is Ming has been well educated, well trained and is very experienced. Until now we were reasonably sure he was dead. One thing is certain: Ming would be a valuable ally for a group like the People's New Guard."

"Any idea what the hell they're doing this for?" McCarter asked, continuing with the reassembling of his KG-99 even as he spoke.

"They think themselves as revolutionaries," Katz replied. "That's the standard excuse for terrorism. They justify it as a revolution to help their people. Kuo Chun clearly feels China has swayed from the path Mao had set. Kuo is trying to turn Westerners against China and the Chinese against Westerners. She's hoping to get the Hui Muslims—and no doubt other groups, especially religious groups—to turn against the Chinese government."

"Why?" Ross asked, clearly confused. "Does that insane bitch think that will bring Mao back to life?"

"She believes it will cause a return to the more restrictive government controls that existed under Mao," Pao explained. "If China breaks off relations with the West, we will surely become an isolationist country again. If turmoil erupts from the Muslim and Buddhist sectors, religions will be abolished. Businesses, farming, everything else will go back to the collectivist system, even if it did fail under Mao's regime. Before long we'd be back to where we were in 1976. It will be as if Mao had come back from the grave to reclaim the seat of power. That's exactly what Kuo wants.''

"And she thinks all that will happen due to these acts of terrorism?" Ross still could not believe it.

"Have you read the *I Ching*?" John Trent asked quietly. As usual, the American ninja had remained silent until he had something to contribute to the conversation.

"The *I Ching*?" Ross stared at him as if he had lost his mind. "You mean that fortune-telling crap? Throw the sticks and see what the future holds?"

"I refer to the text of the *I Ching*, not any mystical practices associated with it," Trent explained. "The *I Ching*, or *Book of Changes*, is possibly the oldest book still used by civilizations to this day. It was in circulation during the year 1100 B.C., and it may be even older than that. At any rate, one of the passages of the *I Ching* speaks of a great shock felt for hundreds of miles. If it creates enough fear, whoever steps forward to offer protection will become a leader."

"That theory has certainly been held up by history," Katz remarked.

"I'm surprised a fanatic like Kuo ever read anything except Mao," Ross muttered.

"Oh, Mao was influenced by the *I Ching*," Pao stated. "Nearly all Chinese philosophers—from Lao-tsu and Confucius—have been influenced by *The Book of Changes*. Virtually all Chinese scholars are familiar with it. With her fanatic zeal, I imagine Kuo Chun regarded this as an ancient bit of wisdom that Mao would have approved of. A major crisis makes people frightened and eager for a leader with quick solutions. So why not make the crisis in the first place?"

"That all makes sense in a demented sort of way," McCarter commented with a nod.

"Then it ought to make sense to you," Manning said dryly. "What about the claim that white terrorists conducted an attack on Chinese civilians in Shanghai? Did you ask Feng about that?"

"Indeed," Pao confirmed. "Feng had the answers, too. He imported some former mercenaries, white Europeans, and a couple of American deserters from the Vietnam conflict. It seems they had all been connected with Triad drug traffickers in Singapore, Thailand and Hong Kong."

"We're talkin' about some real low-life characters, man," James said grimly.

The black badass from Chicago had a personal reason to both find deserters of the Vietnam War contemptible and despise drug dealers on any level. James was a veteran of the Vietnam War. McCarter and Manning had also participated in the Southeast Asian conflict as "special observers," and they had seen a good deal of action and took part in several missions attached to SOG in Nam. Especially Manning, who had honed his skills as a sniper and combat demolitions expert while working with the 5th Special Force.

Yet, it was not the same for them as it had been for the American servicemen who spent their time in the unique hell of Vietnam. Manning and McCarter had been experts, called in to assist in particular operations. They had a special status, unofficial, yet highly respected by the U.S. military and the CIA spooks who ran the Special Observation Group. They had not been part of the day-to-day terror of the bush or patrolling the waters along the coast. They had not known the frustration of being ordered to avoid the enemy, of having to disengage battle because some high brass idiot was playing politics or Washington was trying to figure out how to handle the conflict.

When McCarter and Manning returned home, no crowds had been waiting to condemn them for participating in the war. Canada and Great Britain had not been divided by social outrage on all sides due to the Southeast Asia conflict. It seemed half of America hated the men who fought in Vietnam because they thought the war was "immoral," The other half seemed to hate the Vietnam vets because they "weren't tough enough to win." The two points of view were that the returning vets were "baby killers" or "pot head sissy cowards." That was what veterans of Vietnam had to look forward to when they returned home.

Since James was a black man, he faced another type of vicious label as well. Some regarded him as an "Uncle Tom" because he went off to fight "whitey's war" instead of joining the civil rights struggle for equality at home. Others, mostly whites who were either bigoted or paranoid or both, suspected James was a "militant violence-junkie." James sometimes figured the "good times" about Vietnam had been being shot at by the enemy.

Calvin James had spent his time in Southeast Asia hell, but he had not run out on his buddies. The idea never occurred to him, and it would never have occurred to most of the guys he had served with. About all a soldier or a sailor had to rely on in combat was himself, his equipment and the other guys with him. Anybody who ran out on his pals under those circumstances was a son of a bitch, in James's opinion. He knew how tough it had been in Nam and how things sucked when a vet returned to "the world"—as they used to refer to the United States. Still, that did not excuse abandoning your brothers in the field.

The subject of drugs was another thing that stung more painfully than a branding iron. James had seen the dope dealers hustling poison to kids in the neighborhood he grew up in. The south side of Chicago was a different kind of battlefield. Poverty, despair, anger, disappointment and crime were a way of life in the ghetto. The pushers drove big cars, wore fancy clothes and had lots of women. They bragged about "gettin' over on the Man" and "gettin' a piece of the pie from whitey," but they were selling junk to *black* kids. They were preying on fellow blacks like hungry scorpions cannibalizing one another.

James hated the dealers and pushers as a kid, and he found their breed even more disgusting as an adult. Worst of all, their numbers increased, getting richer and bolder with each passing year. Then James's younger sister died from a drug overdose. She had fallen in with a bad crowd and it cost her her life. His mother was killed the same year, murdered in her own home, probably by junkies looking for something worth stealing. The two tragic events had caused James to turn from pursuing a career in medicine and chemistry to law enforcement. It also left him with a lasting hatred for dope dealers.

The notion of putting pushers *and* deserters out of business appealed to Calvin James. The mission was important enough before, but now it had some extra icing, and James looked forward to savoring the moment when they caught up with the traitorous, poison-peddling trash who had joined forces with the People's New Guard.

"Okay, mates," McCarter began, leaning back in his chair with a can of cola in his hand. "Bottom line: Do we know where the terrorist base is located?"

"Feng said there are actually two bases," Pao answered. "One is located at the Tibetan Plateau."

"Are you sure about that?" Yang asked with an expression of despair. "There's been so much unrest and turmoil in the Tibet portion of the Xizang Zizhiqu region already."

"I'm not surprised," Ross snorted. "China has a rather poor record of human rights for the Tibetans. Don't try to pin all the blame on Mao, either. Things haven't changed that much in the past twelve years. Not in Tibet.''

Yang glared at the CIA agent, staring daggers at Ross as if trying to will the man to topple over dead. Pao cast a hard gaze at the American, although he knew Ross was telling the truth. There had been riots in the Xizang region during the Tibetan New Year in March of 1988. That was hardly a state secret, although Beijing wished it could be.

Katz wished Ross had kept his mouth shut. It was not the time or the place to be criticizing Chinese policies. The Israeli suspected Ross was getting tired of listening to the SAD agents talk about China as if it had been transformed into utopia since Mao's death. Katz even shared Ross's attitude to a degree. There were still strict government controls of publishing, radio and television in the People's Republic. Most of the songs taught to school children were still propaganda slogans set to music with lyrics cheering on the Communist Party and its promise of making every one healthy, happy and wise. China was faced with a crushing problem of overpopulation, which the government combatted by urging couples to have only one child. There were stories—officially unconfirmed—that the attempts at population control included forced sterilization and such late abortions that they almost amounted to infanticide. It was impossible to find out the exact situation in a country engaged in ongoing change. At any rate, issues like that weren't Phoenix Force's current concern.

''Let's not offend our hosts, Mr. Ross,'' Katz said sternly, clicking the steel hooks of his prosthesis to make sure the CIA man understood that he was annoyed with him as well. ''Let's concentrate on the mission. So far, that has given us more than enough to cope with.''

''Sorry,'' Ross said sheepishly. ''I was out of line.''

''Yeah,'' James muttered. ''No shit.''

"The other terrorist base is supposed to be in Shandong," Pao declared, eager to get away from discussions about Tibet. "It's located along the coast of the Yellow Sea. Now, this is the main headquarters, according to Feng. Commander Kuo and her top people are based there. Ming, an explosives and weapons expert named Lin No-su and a super-commando type called Chien are generally at this location with Kuo."

"So let's go get the dirty bleeders," McCarter said eagerly, placing his Coke can on the table a bit harder than he intended to. "We kicked arse at the tong harbor, and we can do it again to the rest of the bastards."

"There will be more terrorists to deal with at the base than you found at the smuggler's harbor," Yang warned. "They will almost certainly be better armed and better prepared for any attack we carry out on their stronghold. I know you had great success against Feng's group, but this will be more difficult."

"We've handled far more difficult situations than the harbor assault in the past," Katz assured him. "But we have another problem, judging from what Mr. Pao learned during interrogation."

"Christ, that figures," McCarter growled. "Well, what is it?"

"Feng said that Kuo and her group have something big planned for tomorrow," Pao explained. "A major terrorist action, bigger than anything they've done before. However, Feng doesn't know where the attack will take place. Apparently Kuo and Ming did not have absolute faith in Feng and his tong. They didn't share many details with him."

"What did they say about the strike?" Manning asked.

"Feng said that none of his white-trash killers will be used," Pao said. "That suggests the target will be either

American or European tourists or a minority group such as the Hui.''

"Or they could try it the other way around,'' Encizo remarked. "They might disguise their terrorists as Hui or Tibetans or whatever and attack Chinese majority sectors.''

"He also said the attack would be against a target which we could not possibly protect with escalated security,'' Pao added. "Feng suspected it was a tourist attraction of some sort, but he did not know which one.''

"A tourist attraction that can't be covered by security personnel,'' Katz said thoughtfully. "That might suggest that it is too large for the police to cover the entire area.''

"Or too long,'' Calvin James commented, thinking the same thing as the Israeli pro.

"Of course,'' Yang declared. "The Wall.''

"Yes,'' Pao said with a nod. "The Great Wall of China is probably our best known historic sight. Certainly it is the largest and the longest. The terrorists may very well be right. The Wall is too enormous for us to protect all the tourists who visit it.''

"The terrorists aren't going to attack the whole damn wall simultaneously,'' Encizo stated. "They can't manage enough manpower to handle that task any more than the police can. You could call in the military. If soldiers were posted all along the Wall, that would probably discourage the terrorists.''

"That would require thousands of troops,'' Pao explained. "SAD has its limits. The Central Committee would have to approve such an action. First I'd have to go through the Central External Liaison Department and then to the Ministry of Defense. Odds are that we still wouldn't manage to get authorization for that many troops fast enough to put them in position along the Wall.''

"The terrorists may call off the attack when they learn Feng was busted," James remarked. "If this Ming guy is as good as you say he is, he probably has sources of information within SAD. It won't take long for them to realize Feng and his tong buddies got rugged. The terrorists will guess Feng told us where the headquarters is located. Unless they're stupid—which they obviously aren't—those dudes ain't gonna hang around. They'll haul ass and set up shop somewhere else."

"I agree," Katz said with a nod. "They will strike their base and go elsewhere to continue operations. However, I doubt that they'll cancel the strike tomorrow."

"Today," Manning corrected, glancing at his Timex chronograph wristwatch. "It's past midnight. In fact it's four in the morning. If the terrorists do launch an attack at the Great Wall, we'd better be ready for them, and there isn't much time."

"Look, we have to bear in mind that we're dealing with extremists who believe in violence as a primary tactic," Katz began. "And they're Maoist extremists. Most of their tactics have been right out of Mao's 'Little Red Book.' To be honest, it has been a while since I read it, but I seem to recall Mao stressed striking at small, poorly defended areas in war situations. To the terrorists, this is a revolutionary war. Mao also said quite a bit about preparing for battles and the intervals between battles, which should be brief. Mao didn't believe in giving the enemy time to catch his breath. You fellows are probably better acquainted with Mao's book than I am. Do you agree, or am I drifting?"

"I doubt that you ever drift much, Mr. Gray," Pao remarked with obvious respect for the Phoenix commander. "And I agree with your observations about the terrorists and the works of Chairman Mao. I think you may be right. The terrorists will strike before they leave their base. To do otherwise would put too long an interval between the last action and the next.''

"So how do we handle it?'' Encizo asked with a massive shrug.

"There are three objectives here,'' Katz began. "The terrorist headquarters, the terrorist base in Tibet and the intended target of the terrorists, which we've decided is probably the Great Wall of China. Let's not fancy ourselves as being above mistakes. We might be wrong about the Wall. Another site may be the target.''

"Security has been doubled or even tripled at every major historic landmark and popular tourist center,'' Yang assured him.

"Those measures need to be checked out and supervised by the best people SAD has available,'' Manning suggested. "We'll have our hands full with the Wall. No way this little group can cover hundreds of miles at the same time.''

"There are parts of the Wall which are visited more frequently by tourists than others,'' Pao explained. "Ancient towers and sections near palaces and other sites. One of these must be the intended target—if indeed our basic assumption is right.''

"We'll have to determine the best way to cover these,'' Katz said. "Meantime, the base in Tibet needs to be taken care of. The terrorists at the headquarters may also be ready to flee, even as their killer team goes into the field.''

The Phoenix Force commander approached a map of the People's Republic. The writing was in Chinese ideographs, and Katz asked Pao to show him where Shandong Province was located on the map.

"Here,'' the SAD agent answered, pointing to a portion of the east coast of China. "This is the Yellow Sea. From what Feng says, the base should be here, near Wendeng.''

"And the Great Wall is inland here, right?" Katz asked, tapping his prosthesis on the line of block-shaped patterns along the map. "About six hundred kilometers from the base?"

"Correct," Pao confirmed. "We may be able to launch a raid on the site and cover the wall at the same time."

"Let's try to block off any escape routes instead," the Israeli suggested. "Patrol boats along the coast. Soldiers at the roads and checking the railroad stations and whatever else they've got there."

"You don't want to be left out of the kill?" Ross asked with a cynical snort.

"I won't deny that," Katz confessed, "but we also want to handle it personally, because Kuo might have other agents and bases we don't know about. If at all possible, we want to save as many of her and Ming's records as possible. We also want to take a few of the top people alive for questioning."

"Then you can hit the base and leave the rest up to the Company and SAD," Ross stated. "CIA hasn't had a very active role in this."

"You weren't handling things too well before we got here," McCarter scoffed. "We have authority over you blokes whether CIA likes it or not. Any objections? You can take 'em up with the man in the Oval Office when you get back to the States."

"So what brilliant plan do you have in mind?" Ross demanded.

"Tourists," Katz supplied the answer.

14

The morning sun shone brightly in the blue-gray sky. Puffs of white clouds drifted gently overhead. It was a pleasant day in northern China. The weather was agreeable, neither too hot nor too cold. It was a perfect day to visit the Great Wall.

Thousands visited the Wall, tourists and native Chinese alike. It was one of the most remarkable man-made wonders in the world. The Great Wall extended from Jinwangdo to Gansu, nearly fifteen hundred miles. The ancient wall had required centuries to complete. Construction began in the year 221 B.C. Emperor Shih Huang Ti had ordered the systematic building of the wall to keep out nomadic barbarians. The Ming Dynasty continued to build onto the Great Wall.

The accomplishment was incredible to behold. Miles and miles of the Wall wound across the countryside like an enormous serpent of stone and brick. The Wall conformed to the valleys, hills and mountains and followed the course of rivers in its path, rather than bridging the waters. The result was a pleasant sight, a remarkable ancient marvel which stood in harmony with the landscape, as if the Wall served as a grand monument to the Taoist ideal of man and nature together in harmony.

The Wall stood twenty-five-feet high and varied in thickness from about twelve feet at the top to as much as thirty feet at the base. The structure was staggering in size and detail. Like the spine of a giant dragon within the earth itself, the Great Wall was a tribute to China and her people. Crumbled at some sections, worn by weather and earthquakes, victimized by war and the passing of centuries, the Wall still stood.

A popular section of the Wall was an ancient watchtower to the north of Beijing. It was actually part of an inner wall section, a sort of secondary defense for the old Imperial Capital. The location of the watchtower made it accessible to tourists visiting the capital city. The site itself was compelling. Located along a mountain range, the Wall extended across an impressive array of scenery. An elevated pathway, paved with stone, provided the means of getting to the tower. Hundreds of stone steps led to the building. Along the wall the average height of watchtowers was approximately forty feet, but the tower near Beijing was more than twice that high.

Thousands of people visited the tower that crisp, clear morning. Yakov Katzenelenbogen, Gary Manning, David McCarter and Mr. Pao had been watching the crowds since shortly after daybreak. Long hours had passed quietly. Tourists shuffled up the ramparts and back again without incident. Foreigners and Chinese citizens enjoyed the visit to the country's most famous landmark. There was nothing sinister or even vaguely suspicious about anyone's behavior that morning.

"I'm beginning to suspect this idea of yours is a total waste," Pao whispered as he stepped next to the weary-looking figure in a wheelchair. "We must have guessed wrong. The Wall isn't the target after all."

"It's still early, Mr. Pao," Katz replied without looking up. "We've still got another hour before we scrap this notion and head for the base.

Pao barely glanced at the Phoenix Force commander. Katz sat in the wheelchair, dressed in a wide-brim straw hat, a white linen jacket and dark sunglasses. A blanket was draped across his lap. It covered his legs and the steel hooks of the prosthesis at the end of his right arm. The blanket also concealed the Uzi submachine gun in his lap. The white hairs of a professionally crafted wig hung from beneath the hat, and a realistic white mustache was attached to Katz's upper lip by spirit gum.

The Israeli's appearance and his whole manner were a masterful deception. He looked like a helpless old man who had suffered a serious stroke or some other crippling experience that had left him largely paralyzed. Pao wondered if Katz had ever considered becoming a stage actor. He guessed "Mr. Gray" would have done quite well in that profession.

Pao wore baggy white trousers and an oversize jacket that helped conceal the T-51 pistol in shoulder leather under his arm. His flowery, multicolored shirt was the type generally associated with Hawaii. A Kodak camera hung from his neck, and he sported a green baseball cap with palm trees on it. The SAD felt foolish, but he had to admit the disguise made him look like an Asian-American tourist.

"I never figured if I visited the Great Wall of China I'd be dressed for a bloody masquerade party," McCarter muttered as he strolled toward the other two men.

The British ace's outfit was similar—baggy trousers, a wrinkled sports coat and a yellow San Diego Chargers T-shirt with a football helmet emblem in the center. His cap displayed SD in gold letters, and he looked out from behind a pair of Foster Grant sunglasses. The bulge of the holstered Browning pistol under his jacket was barely visible.

"Nothing's happening here," McCarter complained. "Maybe the others got better luck."

"They would have contacted us by radio," Pao reminded the Briton. "I'm curious about Major Hsing's forces. They should have reached the Tibetan Plateau by now. Hopefully they found more action than we have.''

"Lucky sods," McCarter said with a sigh. "They get to raid a terrorist base while we stand around here looking like extras posing for a travel brochure. While we're twiddling our thumbs here, the villains at the stronghold in Shandong could be setting out to the Yellow Sea in a beautiful pea green boat.''

"The patrols will stop them if they try to escape by sea," Pao commented.

"Don't count on it," McCarter said sourly. "There are patrols to stop smugglers from bringing opium into the country, too, but Feng and his tong goons managed to get past them. I really think we drew a blank here. If we don't move, we're going to lose Kuo, Ming and all the rest of the big fish.''

"We'll wait a little while longer," Katz insisted. "What time is it?''

"It's 11:20," the Briton answered, consulting his Le Gran wristwatch. "Figure we should wait till noon for the lunch crowd to show up?''

"We generally have larger tourist crowds in the afternoon," Pao admitted. "But the terrorist incidents have cut down the tourism in the People's Republic. I don't know if the crowds will be appreciably bigger later in the day, but I have to agree, we can't afford to wait here much longer.''

"A tour bus is scheduled to arrive at 11:15," Katz stated, glancing up at the tower above the stone stairs. "It picks up passengers from the Beijing Hotel. The terrorists might be waiting for it to get here.''

"They picked a fine day to be late," McCarter complained.

"I'm sure they didn't do it on purpose," Katz replied dryly.

Pao sighed and headed up the stone stairs to the watch-tower. McCarter stayed near Katz, pretending to admire the view of Beijing from the footpath. The Briton did not want to stray too far from his partner, because his KG-99 was stored in a knapsack attached to the backrest of Katz's wheelchair. A small two-way radio unit was also packed in the canvas bag. McCarter stared down at the parking area below. Dozens of vehicles were already parked there. Among them was a dark green van which contained a SAD surveillance crew. Gary Manning was down there, too, but McCarter did not see the Canadian moving among the figures that shuffled to and from the Wall.

Then a red-and-white bus appeared on the road. It was a British-style double-decker vehicle. The roofless top level was loaded with passengers, the majority of whom appeared to be American and European tourists. McCarter felt his expectations rise as the rig pulled into the lot. Maybe the day would prove worthwhile after all.

"THE BUS HAS ARRIVED," the voice of a Social Affairs Department agent spoke to Gary Manning via the earphone hooked to his left ear.

The Canadian wore a mock hearing aid, which was actually a radio receiver. In fact the hearing in his left ear was less acute than that of his right. If he continued to use explosives on a regular basis, Manning might need a hearing aid for real; but he would worry about that when the time came. He had elected to wear the receiver plug in his left ear in order to leave his good ear undisturbed by radio static. Manning figured it was more important to hear sounds surrounding him than reports from the guys in the surveillance vehicle, especially if all they had to tell him was something he could see for himself.

"I know," Manning whispered into a miniature microphone clipped to the inside of his jacket lapel. "Stay alert to what else is going on. I'll cover the bus."

Manning shuffled through the crowd and approached the bus. There were so many people it was nearly impossible to watch all of them. Relatively few uniformed police were in the area. A few Chinese paratroopers in plain clothes were also present, but they were inexperienced in intrigue or subversive warfare. They were superb fighters, skilled in small arms and hand-to-hand combat, but they knew next to nothing about recognizing enemies in the guise of harmless fellow countrymen instead of the uniforms of a foreign nation.

The tourists began to file out of the bus. Men, women and a few children stepped from the vehicle. Nearly all appeared to be American or Europeans. They stared up at the Great Wall of China with astonishment. Cameras worked away amid general expressions of wonder. However, Manning paid little attention to the tourists. They were the intended target, not the enemy.

Manning was more interested in the group of Chinese who appeared behind the tourists. There was nothing obviously suspicious about them, yet the veteran Phoenix pro sensed something about the four men the instant he caught sight of them. Manning trusted his instincts. His so-called "sixth sense" had been developed since he was a young man hunting deer in British Columbia. It had served him well in Vietnam and later when he was attached to the West German GSG-9 antiterrorist squad in Europe. Since he joined Phoenix Force, Manning's instincts had saved his life and the lives of others on countless occasions.

It was sending a strong signal to him that moment as he watched the four Asians slowly approach the tour bus. Perhaps it was their manner of dress. All wore loose fitting jackets, similar to what Manning himself wore to conceal the shoulder holster rig with a pistol under his arm. Maybe the way they avoided looking at the tourists had sparked Manning's suspicions. The four men seemed to glance casually in all directions except toward the bus and its passengers. Two of them carried plain brown attaché cases that swung easily in a relaxed manner, yet their knuckles were white from a very tight grip. Although they tried to appear calm, lines of tension still betrayed their features.

"Heads up, everybody," Manning spoke into his lapel mike. "I think things are going to heat up. Tell Gray and the others to be ready. This could be a false alarm, but something tells me otherwise."

"Affirmative," the voice of the SAD guy replied in Manning's left ear.

Manning noticed the four suspicious figures move to the side of the bus. The Canadian hurried to the opposite side of the vehicle, weaving past the tourists as he headed for the bus at a quick walk. Manning reached the front tire by the open doors of the rig. The driver barely glanced at Manning. He seemed weary and more interested in filling out his log than checking on what was going on outside his vehicle. The Canadian bent over and looked under the bus.

One of the brown briefcases had been placed on the ground. A foot at the opposite side of the vehicle shoved the case forward, farther beneath the bus. The action was clearly deliberate. Manning had seen enough incidents of terrorist sabotage to recognize it in progress. He continued on and slipped his hand inside his jacket to seize the grips of the Walther P-5 under his arm.

At the rear of the bus he nearly ran right into one of the four mysterious Chinese men. Probably a lookout for the other members of the team, the man was as surprised as Manning by the unexpected encounter and quickly reached inside his jacket for a weapon. Manning drew his Walther pistol first and chopped the butt across the other man's forearm as the Asian drew his handgun. The blow jarred the Portuguese M-908 from the Chinese gunman's hand.

The man's other hand swiftly snared Manning's wrist above the Walther P-5 and shoved the pistol toward the sky. Manning balled his free hand into a fist and swung a punch at the Asian's head. The man raised his bruised forearm to block the punch. Then he lashed out and delivered a short, hard chop to Manning's collarbone.

The Phoenix fighter hissed through clenched teeth from the sharp pain of the blow, but he retaliated by thrusting his gun hand forward to bash the steel butt of the P-5 into the Asian's mouth. His opponent's head bounced from the blow and blood trickled from a split lip. The man was large for a Chinese, nearly as tall as Manning and thickly muscled. He held on to the Canadian's wrist to keep him from using the gun and rammed a knee into Manning's abdomen.

Manning gasped, and his opponent shoved the Phoenix commander against the bus. Recovering, the Canadian hooked a punch under the man's ribs and followed with an elbow stroke to the upper arm. The combination weakened the Chinese thug and knocked him off balance. He staggered slightly but remained on his feet. Manning thrust his arm violently and broke free of the other man's grasp to swing the pistol barrel across his opponent's jaw.

The big Chinese fell backward and landed on his rump as another Asian killer appeared from the side of the bus, a dagger in his fist. The second thug had heard the scuffle and rushed forward with a blade instead of a gun because he hoped to do his dispatching as silently as possible. He did not realize Manning had a gun until he saw the Walther pistol pointed at his stomach. The knife artist froze in his tracks and stared at the gun, uncertain whether to throw down his dagger or try to rush the Phoenix pro.

Manning shifted the aim of his P-5 and squeezed the trigger. The pistol roared like a stick of dynamite in the deceptively peaceful setting. A 9 mm parabellum slug tore into the knife-man's biceps muscle and shattered the bone beneath. The man screamed and dropped his dagger. He slapped his other hand to the wounded limb and stumbled forward. Unintentionally the injured man stepped into the line of fire as one of his comrades tried to take out Gary Manning with a Type 51 autoloader.

The terrorist's pistol barked twice. Both 7.65 mm slugs slammed into the back of the unlucky knife lover. The reports of the second pistol shots were muffled by the shouts and screams of terror, which erupted from the crowd of tourists and innocent Chinese civilians who suddenly realized danger and death had arrived at the Great Wall. The fellow who stopped the two T-51 rounds was especially aware of this as he fell to the ground, his spinal cord severed and one lung punctured.

Manning had dropped to one knee when he realized a third opponent had opened fire. He held the Walther P-5 in both hands and swung the pistol around the corner of the bus. The man with the T-51 stood dumbfounded, his eyes still locked in disbelief on the body of the comrade he had accidentally killed. Manning did not give the gunman a chance to improve his marksmanship. The Canadian aimed the Walther at his chest and fired two shots. The bullets struck left of center. Both parabellums punched through the Asian triggerman's heart. The terrorist toppled over like a tenpin knocked down by a 115-grain hollow-point bowling ball.

"Shang di!" Lin No-su gasped as he saw his comrades fall lifeless before his horrified eyes.

The Chinese explosives expert was no hero by anyone's definition. Lin No-su had not wanted to participate in the terrorist strike at the Great Wall, but he had been more frightened of Commander Kuo than the authorities. She had insisted he personally plant the explosive charge at the site. He had hoped to do the job and flee the area before the fireworks occurred. Fate had pissed on his hopes, and he found himself face-to-face with an armed opponent.

Lin still held one briefcase in a pudgy fist as he pulled a compact Glock 19 semiautomatic pistol from shoulder leather. He was a paradox in many ways, a nervous man who handled explosives, and a coward knowledgeable in small arms. Lin had chosen the Glock because it was a highly dependable weapon with eighteen-round capacity, not because it was a "plastic gun." He'd heard about the claims by some misinformed individuals in the U.S. Senate and Congress that the Glock could pass through metal detectors and knew it to be completely false because of the pistol's eighteen steel parts. But even the best-made firearms don't include instant courage or skill for the owner, and Lin No-su had little of either attribute.

Manning swung the Walther toward Lin. The Asian promptly dropped his Glock pistol as if it were suddenly red-hot. He released the valise as well and held both empty hands overhead in surrender. Manning gestured with the P-5 to signal Lin to step away from the discarded weaponry. The Chinese nodded and obeyed instructions, his portly body showing visible signs of trembling.

Gary Manning rose, his pistol still trained on Lin No-su. A blur of movement caught his attention via the corner of an eye. Manning whirled to face the attacker. A rock-hard hand chopped his forearm and struck the Walther autoloader from his grasp. The big Asian whom Manning had previously knocked down had gotten to his feet and launched another attack. The terrorist's mouth bled, and an ugly purple bruise marred the side of his jaw, but the flaming anger in his dark eyes revealed that he still had plenty of fight left.

A roundhouse heel-of-the-palm stroke caught Manning on the right cheekbone and knocked him three feet. The Canadian's head was violently jarred with the blow, and lights popped painfully inside his head, yet he managed to stay on his feet. The big Asian swung a kick for the Phoenix crusader's groin, but Manning's hands swooped forward and grabbed the attacker's ankle in midair.

He growled like an angry beast and yanked on the leg to force the Asian off balance. The terrorist hopped awkwardly on his other foot and waved his arms clumsily in an attempt to stay upright. Manning suddenly charged forward and drove a shoulder into the Asian's chest. The force of the blow sent the big Chinese hurtling against the bus.

The terrorist gasped breathlessly as the wind was driven from his lungs. Manning swung a hard uppercut to the opponent's solar plexus, making his opponent wheeze and double up with a groan. Manning glanced at Lin No-su and saw the fat man reach for the Glock pistol on the ground. The Canadian grabbed his battered opponent's shirtfront with one hand and jammed the other between the man's legs. Manning hauled the big Chinese off his feet in a modified crotch-lift. The man uttered a breathless groan as the pressure in his groin choked off his cries.

Manning pulled with one arm and pushed with the other. He released the Asian, sending him hurtling into Lin No-su like a human cannonball. Both men tumbled to the ground in a moaning, dazed heap. Manning quickly scooped up his Walther pistol, but neither opponent was in any condition to offer any further threat. The Canadian heard screams, shouts, an array of semiauto and full-auto gunshots accompanied by the thunder of thousands of footsteps. All hell was breaking loose at the Great Wall.

The Phoenix Force demolitions expert tried to block out the sounds of battle and panic. He had another task to deal with that was just as important. Manning reached under the bus and retrieved the valise placed beneath the vehicle. He knelt by the case and carefully examined it for booby traps. Manning reached into a jacket pocket and removed a small leather packet.

He unzipped the container, his hands steady although his heart began to race. The Canadian explosives genius knew better than anyone the risk involved. There are a thousand ways to rig explosives and a thousand and one ways to booby-trap a briefcase to blow up in a person's face. There was no way he could be sure the case was one hundred percent safe before he opened it.

Manning removed a teakwood letter opener from the packet and carefully inserted the wood blade into the crack between the frame and the lid. A metal blade might spark against metal inside the case or sever sensitive wires to detonate a rigged charge. The wood blade was less hazardous, although the danger was still great. Manning felt the tension build as he slowly worked the letter opener along the hinged portion of the case. He avoided the latches by the handle. If the briefcase was rigged, it would probably be wired to the lock.

He tried not to think about everything that could go wrong, but his vast knowledge of explosives worked against him in this regard. The lid could be lined with plastic explosives and attached to a pressure-plate detonator that would blow up if the lid budged a centimeter. A crisscrossing of filament wiring on the interior of the case would make it impossible to open without setting off the bomb. A mercury temperature gauge, attached to the explosives, could trigger the charge if the temperature rose an iota of a degree. Even the warmth of a human finger or the friction caused by the wood blade could be enough to detonate the explosive surprise within the attaché case.

Well, Manning thought with grim philosophy, if it blows I'll be dead so fast I probably won't feel a thing. However, the probe did not locate any wires near the hinges. Manning used the letter opener and a pair of pliers to pry loose the rivets at the foot of the case. Carefully he worked on the hinges until he freed them from the shell of the valise. Manning sprawled on his belly as he eased the case open with the blade of the wood knife. He switched on a small pocket flashlight and peered inside.

Two packs of yellow-orange putty, roughly the size of cigarette packs, were taped to the base of the case shell. C-3 plastic explosives, Manning realized. Enough to blow up everybody and everything in the parking area. The C-3 was wired to a small digital clock-timer with a plug attachment hooked to the detonator. It was a simple explosive, a standard time bomb. He eased the case open and reached in with the pliers. Manning gripped the plug in the teeth of the pliers and gently pulled it from the clock. Then he snipped the wires. The bomb was deactivated.

Manning allowed himself a sigh of relief, but he could not spend too much time congratulating himself. He had another briefcase to take care of—and no doubt, another bomb inside. It was probably rigged exactly as the first had been, but Manning realized he could not risk making any assumptions when dealing with sabotage devices. So he gathered up the second attaché case and began the entire nerve-racking process all over again.

WHEN THE FIRST SHOTS were fired, other terrorists responded as if called to action by a prearranged signal. Men appeared from parked vehicles, clad in coveralls, gloves, hats and scarf-style masks. They carried T-56 rifles, T-50 submachine guns and an assortment of other weapons of Taiwanese and Portuguese design. A couple of them toted British-made firearms imported from Hong Kong. However, Katz, McCarter and their Chinese allies had also been alerted by the shooting and sprang into action.

A terrorist with a subgun promptly trained his weapon on a startled policeman who was still trying to draw a pistol from the button-flap holster on his hip. The enemy gunman blasted a column of 7.65 mm slugs across the policeman's chest before the officer could draw his side arm. David McCarter saw the terrorist murder the policeman from the base of the tower steps, about a hundred feet above the lot.

"Bloody bastard," the British ace growled as he gripped his Browning Hi-Power in both hands and aimed at the killer below.

Most pistol shooters would have found the shot difficult, but McCarter did not hesitate, confident of his hard-earned skill and battle-honed instincts. He triggered the Browning, and a 9 mm round crashed into the top of the terrorist's skull. The man fell to his knees, the T-50 still gripped in his fists. He was already dead when he dropped forward and landed face-first on the ground.

Another enemy gunman saw his comrade fall and glanced about for the source of his companion's death. He looked up and saw McCarter aim the Browning over the top of the low wall along the walkway to the watchtower. Too late, the man realized he was McCarter's next target. He raised his T-56 rifle as the Briton fired his pistol. The bullet smashed through the terrorist's forehead before he could trigger his weapon, and he collapsed just as two others took up his cause and fired their weapons at McCarter's position.

The Briton ducked behind the stone ridge of the wall. Bullets whined against the barrier and chipped the top of the low wall. McCarter stayed down low as he hurried for cover farther along the pathway. Tourists and civilians screamed and ran in pandemonium along the walkway, panicked by the shooting. McCarter corralled several passersby and urged them to seek cover and damn well stay there until the shooting was over.

Chinese paratroopers and SAD agents confronted the terrorists in the parking area. The majority of the Social Affairs Department boys were not very experienced with firearms and gun battles. They fired their pistols to little effect, either spending too much time trying to aim, or shooting haphazardly without a definite target. The paratroopers, however, had spent years preparing for such combat. The soldiers were far more accurate with their weapons than either the SAD agents or the terrorists.

The New Guard killers had received crash courses in murder and mayhem with a lot of Maoist propaganda lectures. They were not too impressive against opponents who could fight back. Several terrorists were cut down by the paratroopers and SAD agents. They returned fire. One Social Affairs Department snoop expert failed to reach cover fast enough and went down with three bullets in his chest. A paratrooper also caught a slug in the left thigh before he reached shelter behind a parked automobile. Others fired back at the aggressors from cover positions behind parked vehicles and rest room structures.

Terrorists continued to be cut down. Two of them rushed to the bus for shelter. They ran around the nose of the rig and found Gary Manning waiting for them. The Canadian fired his Walther pistol and pumped two 9 mm slugs into the upper torso and neck of the nearest opponent. The other terrorist bolted away from Manning and ducked around the front of the vehicle. He was spotted by a paratrooper who nailed him three times in the center of the chest.

More terrorists appeared at the tower itself. Originally disguised as South Korean businessmen with name tags pinned to the lapels of their suits, they had whipped out gloves, ski masks and weapons from their attaché cases and launched the second prong of the attack. Tourists cried out in terror as the gunmen threatened them with an assortment of machine pistols and semiauto handguns.

Mr. Pao stepped inside the stone walls of the ancient watchtower as three masked gunmen herded the civilians into a group against a wall and two others headed up the stone steps to the top of the tower above. Pao put his hands behind his head. The barrel of his T-51 pistol was inserted into the back collar of his jacket. His head and his left hand concealed the weapon in his right fist from the view of the terrorist gunmen.

"Wei shenme?" Pao asked as he stepped forward. "Why? Why are you doing this?"

"Guan zui!" a terrorist snapped and pointed a Russian-made Stechkin machine pistol at the SAD agent. "Shut up! Move there, with the others!"

"All right," Pao replied and slowly backed away from the gunman to move toward the hostages.

A wheelchair, propelled along by the old man sitting in it, rolled into view at the entrance of the tower. The terrorists were surprised by the newcomer. The disabled man calmly stopped his chair and slipped his left hand under the blanket in his lap as he looked up at the terrorists and smiled stupidly, apparently unaware of what was going on.

"Senile white piece of shit!" the killer with the Stechkin hissed as he turned his weapon toward the wheelchair.

Pao's arm snapped forward, T-51 pistol in his fist. He fired the gun point-blank at the gunman's head. A 7.65 mm slug tore into the killer's right temple and blasted a lethal tunnel into his brain. The other two terrorists were taken off guard by Pao's actions, and were slow to react. They started to swing their weapons toward the SAD agent.

Yakov Katzenelenbogen threw off the blanket as he hopped out of the wheelchair. The Uzi submachine gun was braced across his prosthesis, pointed at the terrorist pair.

He triggered a three-round burst and blasted the closest opponent in the chest. The man went down with a spill of blood from his bullet-punctured heart.

Unnerved by the unexpected double threat of Katz and Pao, the third gunman was uncertain which opponent to cope with first. He swung his Sterling chopper toward Katz, but the Israeli's Uzi spoke first. Pao opened fire virtually the same instant as the Phoenix commander. Three 9 mm Uzi rounds slammed into the terrorist's torso, and two 7.65 mm slugs struck his face and ripped into his brain. The New Guard killer was done for, and the Sterling machine gun clattered next to its slain owner. Pao rushed forward and gathered up the British-made blaster.

"Two more upstairs!" the SAD agent exclaimed as he ran to the stairs.

Katz started to gallop up the stone steps behind Pao, followed by a swelling chorus from the civilians, expressions of outrage and horror along with relief and joy for being still alive. Several demanded to know what the hell was going on. The Phoenix pro and his SAD companion ignored them. Lives were still in jeopardy, and that was more important than satisfying the curiosity of those no longer in danger.

Pao reached the top of the stairs first. Shots were already being fired from the roof, and screams echoed above the stairwell. The SAD man stepped onto the roof of the tower and saw two terrorist gunmen standing near the bloodied corpses of three dead tourists. Two men and a woman lay sprawled on the stone surface, their bleeding flesh riddled by bullets. The amount of blood along the edge of the roof suggested at least one other innocent victim had been murdered, but the body had fallen over the side.

Pao snarled with anger and loathing at the sight of the butchery. The terrorists prepared to open fire on six other helpless civilian hostages. Pao pointed his T-51 at the closest terrorist and fired two rounds into the man's back. The 7.65 mm projectiles punched the killer between the shoulder blades. He cried out in agony and twisted around from the impact, a Portuguese M-976 submachine gun in his fists. The terrorist's mouth hung open, blood drooling from his lips. Still he managed to trigger his weapon.

A stream of 9 mm slugs slashed across Pao's upper body. A bullet shattered his right shoulder, another splintered his breastbone, and a third struck him high in the left side of his chest. Pao moaned as the pistol dropped from his quivering fingers. His body burned with white-hot pain, and his shoulder felt as if it was filled with broken glass. His chest seemed to have been skewered by a sizzling-hot railroad spike. Pao's eyes blurred, but he saw the man who shot him. The terrorist had collapsed to the roof and thrashed about in mindless agony. Pao's bullets had split the killer's backbone.

The other terrorist fired his Stechkin machine pistol. One more burst of high-velocity missiles smashed into Pao's chest. He fell backward and tumbled down the stairwell. Katzenelenbogen dodged the falling body and charged to the top, his Uzi held ready. The terrorist with the Stechkin had turned his weapon on the remaining tourists. Katz snap-aimed and triggered his Uzi. The wave of 9 mm parabellums blasted the terrorist and sent him hurtling over the cresting. The man screamed as he plunged from the tower, to land on the hard earth nearly a hundred feet below.

"Oh, my God!" a nearly hysterical woman sobbed as she huddled beside a pair of children cowering in mute fear. "Is it over?"

"As far as you need to worry about it," Katz assured her as he approached the body of the other terrorist. He made certain the man was dead and confiscated the M-976 subgun from the corpse. "You'll be safe. Just wait here until we're sure the battle's over."

The Israeli headed back down the stairwell. The broken, blood-splattered body of Mr. Pao lay at the foot of the steps. Katz knelt beside him and checked for a pulse. There was a slim, almost nonexistent possibility that Pao might still be alive. Katz had just grimly confirmed his worst fear for the man when David McCarter appeared at the threshold to the tower.

"It's all wrapped up, mates," the Briton announced before he saw Pao's mangled form. "Oh, Jesus. Is he dead?"

"Yes," Katz answered regretfully. "Mr. Pao, or whatever his real name may have been, was a good man. He died bravely. Maybe if I'd gone up the stairs first . . ."

"Maybe if pigs had wings they'd be called pork hawks," McCarter stated. "There's nothing we can do for Pao except see this mission through to the end. I think he'd want us to finish it."

"You're damn right we'll finish it," Katz replied with a firm nod. "Let's see to that right now."

15

Commander Kuo Chun had few personal possessions. She regarded materialism as a crime against the state. The desire for personal property was a terrible flaw in human character, in Kuo's opinion. Therefore it did not take her long to pack her belongings. Some clothing, a photograph of her beloved parents and a framed picture of Chairman Mao, three books, some eating utensils and a T-51 pistol with a spare magazine filled her small duffel bag. Kuo emerged from her quarters, the bag slung over a shoulder.

The stronghold was filled with frenzied activity. Members of the People's New Guard hurried through the corridors, carrying bags and weapons. Ming Ssu approached Kuo, pushing past the others in his haste to talk to her. His expression suggested he was not the bearer of good news.

"We received a radio message from our base in Tibet," Ming explained grimly. "They were under attack. Soldiers had surrounded the site and struck from all sides. Because we did not receive another report, it appears our people at that base were defeated. We must assume the enemy has captured the camp."

"They must have forced Feng to talk," Kuo said, shaking her head with dismay. "That fool allowed himself to be taken alive, and they broke that stinking coward son of a she-pig. I never did trust the gangster. Now I see that I was a fool to ever allow him into our ranks. The tong are capitalists by nature and profession. They were corruption in our camp."

"This is hardly the time for lectures, Comrade Commander," Ming snapped. "The enemy has seized our base in Tibet and the news from an observation post in Beijing is even more distressing. The strike at the Great Wall has failed. Apparently a few foreign tourists, some soldiers, a policeman or two and some Chinese—either civilians or SAD agents—were killed or injured. However, none of our people escaped."

"The bombs!" Kuo rasped, eyes wild like a cornered beast. "Lin No-su told me those bombs had enough explosives to kill hundreds of people."

"The bombs did not explode," Ming stated. "We don't have enough information to know what went wrong. Maybe they found the bombs and deactivated them. Maybe the detonators failed."

"Or Lin failed," Kuo hissed. "That coward may have abandoned the mission and left his comrades to fend for themselves. I wouldn't be surprised if he was a traitor from the beginning. Feng and Lin both betrayed us. Am I surrounded by vipers within my own command?"

"Commander!" Ming said sharply. "We have to think clearly and act quickly. No one was a traitor. No one was a double agent working for the SAD or CIA. If that had been the case we never would have gotten as far as we have."

"Why should I believe you?" Kuo glared at the former SAD agent. "The assault on the tourists at the Wall was your idea. Feng didn't know any details about that. How did they know about the Wall unless you told them?"

"The security at the Great Wall was greater than we imagined," Ming answered, trying to calm her. "Maybe they suspected the watchtower at Beijing would be a likely target because it is so close to the capital and very popular with tourists. I don't know the answers, Comrade. If I did,

I would have to be privy to such information that only a traitor would know. What matters now is that we get out of here.''

"If they attacked our team at the Wall and our base in Tibet," Kuo began, her eyes shifting back and forth as a crooked smile crept across her lips, "why didn't they attack here as well? Perhaps they don't even know about this base!''

"If they learned about the other operations, they know about this headquarters as well," Ming insisted, getting frustrated with Kuo. "We should have already left. We certainly can't wait any longer. There will be sea patrols and roadblocks set up by now. At any rate, it is best we assume that has happened.''

"How do we get past these blockades?'' Kuo demanded.

"I've already seen to that,'' Ming assured her. "Some of our more expendable personnel will be sent out to sea. The patrol boats will encounter them. Others will drive vehicles to the west and will come upon the roadblocks. While the enemy is busy with these expendable forces, the rest of us will escape to the north. We'll disguise ourselves as farm workers and travel on foot to avoid the roads. It is still risky, of course, but it is our best chance.''

"And we sacrifice our comrades to save ourselves?'' Kuo sneered and spat with disgust. "Do you value your skin so highly you would allow eighty other lives to be lost to protect it?''

Actually, that was exactly how Ming Ssu felt. He would have willingly let eighty or eighty thousand die if it meant he could survive. But of course, he would not admit that to Kuo Chun. Ming lowered his head and shook it slowly, apparently distressed by Kuo's accusation.

"I would sacrifice my life gladly for our cause,'' Ming told her, hoping she believed his lie. "I would give up my life to save our comrades—if it would help our cause. Sadly this is not the case. The opposite is true. You and I must go on if we are ever to restore China to the pure state of true Communism under the banner of Chairman Mao. We are leaders. The people will be our army. The people are waiting for leaders like us to save our country from the poison of the Western capitalists. I would sacrifice my life, your life and the lives of a thousand others to achieve that goal.''

"Comrade Ming," Kuo began, placing a hand on his shoulder. She nodded as she peered into his eyes, an expression of sympathy on her broad features. "I have listened and I must say this . . ."

She suddenly rammed a knee into his groin. Ming gasped from the hot pain that shot up from between his legs. Kuo hooked her hand around the back of Ming's head as she turned sharply. She thrust her arm forward and tripped Ming with an extended leg. He pitched forward into a wall and fell awkwardly to all fours.

"You're a liar!" she snarled with contempt.

Several New Guard followers rushed forward to see what was going on. Ming stared up at the surprised faces of the onlookers. Chien was among them. The commando leader smiled with amusement, pleased that Kuo had humiliated the former SAD agent in front of witnesses. Ming's anger boiled inside him like hot lava about to explode, but self-control was one of his greatest attributes. So was self-preservation. If he killed Kuo now, the others—especially Chien—would tear him to pieces.

"Try that...again...when I'm not caught...off guard," Ming began, gingerly holding himself with one hand as he slowly got to his feet. "You would...then be the one on the floor, Comrade Commander."

"I doubt that," Kuo replied. She did not intend to let Ming save face. "Your tactics of cowardice make you less than a man. Indeed, it appears you are also less than a woman."

The crowd chuckled at this remark. Ming wanted to smash in her face or draw his pistol and kill her that very moment. But he saw Chien's hand resting on the hilt of his sword. If Ming reached for the gun, Chien would chop his arm before he could draw his pistol. He would simply have to endure the ridicule and plan his revenge later.

"We will all leave as planned," Kuo declared. "None of our comrades will be sacrificed to help save you from danger. Is that understood, Comrade Ming?"

"I understand you are a fool, Commander," Ming answered, meeting Kuo's glare with his own. "You're not going to save anyone by this heroic gesture. Instead you'll get us all killed."

"Traitor!" Chien hissed as he drew the sword from its scabbard. The long blade rose over Chien's head. He grabbed the handle in a firm two-hand grip.

Ming flinched. He recoiled and his back touched the wall. Chien held the sword ready, waiting for Kuo to order him to execute Ming Ssu. The renegade SAD agent's fingers moved reflexively toward the T-51 autoloader on his hip, but he stopped himself, aware that Chien's sword could deliver a lethal stroke before he could clear leather.

"Put your sword away," Kuo ordered. "It's not the time to fight among ourselves. If we are to survive, we must be strong and united. Chairman Mao said it is imperative to overcome anything that impairs our unity."

She fixed a hard gaze on Ming's face and asked, "Will you impair our unity, or will you stand with us?"

"My survival obviously depends on doing what you say," Ming replied. "That should insure you of my loyalty even if you don't trust my sense of dedication to the cause."

"That shall have to do," Kuo stated with a nod. "For now at least. We need to—"

The roar of an explosion interrupted her remark. The building trembled from the blast, and some of the terrorists staggered off balance, swung about with weapons in search of unseen attackers or simply froze in place with stunned expressions plastered across their faces. Kuo stared in the direction of the explosion. Chien pivoted, sword still held overhead.

"I think our choices have just been drastically cut, Commander," Ming declared with a slight smile, more ironic than amused.

"If circumstances force us to fight," Kuo replied, again turning the the *Quotations of Mao Tse-tung* as her inspiration, "then we shall fight to the finish!"

THE LAN-LUNG HELICOPTER circled the old factory below. The chopper was a newly developed addition to the People's Republic military forces. The gunship was equipped with plenty of firepower. It packed two mounted machine guns at the nose and four rockets under the carriage. The Lan-Lung was large enough to carry fourteen passengers, plus pilot and copilot. The chopper was filled to capacity, and they were all ready to fight.

Yakov Katzenelenbogen, Gary Manning and David McCarter were among the men inside the cabin. They had not even had time to change into full combat uniform before they flew from the Great Wall in Beijing to the Shandong Province. All three Phoenix Force commandos had donned boots and field jackets as well as ammo belts with extra magazines for weapons and grenades. Manning was once again armed with his FAL assault rifle and carried a field pack of explosives.

SAD Agent Yang and Chinese paratroopers comprised the rest of the passengers and crew. All were armed with T-50 submachine guns, T-51 side arms, grenades and an assortment of knives. They appeared to be as determined as the Phoenix trio felt. Yang had seen the body of Mr. Pao before it was carted away at the Great Wall. He had barely uttered a word since they boarded the gunship except to say, "Let's get the rest of the bastards."

The factory below was an old abandoned building—officially, anyway. It had formerly been a fishing cannery, but the local fish had been contaminated by a chemical spill off the coast eight years before, so the factory had been closed and workers transferred to a new cannery farther down the coast. The old one had been virtually ignored ever since— ignored by everyone except Kuo Chun and the People's New Guard terrorists.

A missile had been fired near the front entrance of the building to discourage the terrorists from trying to leave the factory by that route. The blast shattered windows and bowled over some barrels in front of the building. Two sentries, posted at the front, were also knocked down by the explosion. Their bodies were sprawled, torn and bloodied, on the ground. If they were still alive, they would not be in any shape to put up a fight.

"Have the pilot lower the copter over the roof," Katz instructed as he pulled open the sliding door to the cabin. "About six meters from the roof, if he can manage it and still hover as steady as possible."

"I could bloody well manage it," McCarter commented. "Well, I *probably* could if I was familiar with this type of aircraft. The Blue Dragon is a new one to me."

"Blue Dragon?" Manning asked with raised eyebrows.

"Lan-Lung," Yang explained. "It means 'blue dragon' in English. The dragon is an important part of Chinese folklore. Europeans generally regarded their dragons as evil, while we Asians viewed the dragon as a great, powerful force of nature. There are dragons of the earth, dragons of the sea, and of course, dragons of the sky."

"Well, this dragon seems to spit fire pretty accurately," Katz commented, raising his voice to be heard above the roar of rotor blades as he knelt by the open sliding door. "Just tell them to be careful with those rockets. We don't want the building to cave in on us after we get inside. After we get to the roof, have them swing the chopper around and fire some volleys at the first-story windows for a diversion long enough to let us make our move."

"And keep an eye on the pier and the junk in the dock," McCarter added. "The blokes out there might be armed with some rocket launchers and such of their own."

"I thought our friends were taking care of that," Yang remarked.

"Cover your ass," Manning told him. "First rule of any military operation. You cover your own butt and don't rely on anybody else to do it for you. If the second team is on schedule, we'll know soon enough. Meantime, don't take anything for granted."

"Don't worry," Yang assured him. "Good luck, gentlemen."

"We can all use some," McCarter admitted.

16

The rope ladder dangled from the Lan-Lung chopper as it hovered over the roof of the main building of the factory. David McCarter climbed down the rungs first. The wind whipped the Briton's clothing and hair. He glanced down at the box-shaped metalworks section where sheet tin had once been cut and formed into cans before being delivered to the main building where fish were carved up and packed into the containers and sealed. It had once been a pretty ambitious project for a fairly small setup. The terrorists who occupied the factory since were far more ambitious and extremely dangerous.

The ladder swayed as McCarter descended, KG-99 on a shoulder strap, Browning Hi-Power in shoulder leather under his arm and other weapons and accessories attached to his belt. The Phoenix pro saw figures move along the deck of the junk docked at the pier. He could not see them clearly, but they appeared to be armed. More shapes stirred near the big scrap bins by the metalworks shop. McCarter felt the usual rush of tension and excitement as he continued to climb down the rope ladder.

"This makes Operation Nimrod look bloody tame," he commented through clenched teeth, but his mouth was locked in a grimace which resembled a nervous smile. "This is the sort of thing I joined Phoenix Force for. Maybe I am crazy."

Automatic fire erupted. McCarter instinctively ducked his head and clung tightly to the rungs. The heat of projectiles sliced air near his neck. He felt his stomach knot as more full-auto weapons roared. Something struck the top of his head. The Briton gasped and nearly lost his grip on the ladder, but the object did not strike with the velocity and bone-crushing force of a bullet. Something else tapped him on the shoulder. It felt as if a giant raindrop had landed on him, or perhaps a big hailstone.

Another salvo of automatic fire snarled, and McCarter felt more of the mysterious "hailstones." One landed inside his collar. Initial contact with the small hot metal cylinder next to his bare skin made McCarter wince, but then he nearly laughed out loud. God, he knew what it was now. He had been around enough full- and semiauto weapons to have had spent cartridge casings fall inside his shirt before. The brass shells were falling from the helicopter, ejected from an automatic rifle fired at the enemy gunmen below.

McCarter glanced up. Gary Manning leaned out of the open cabin door, FAL rifle in one hand, butt stock braced to a brawny shoulder. His other hand gripped a harness strap to keep his balance as he peered through the Bushnell scope and fired at the figures at the bins. Most men could not hit an elephant at ten paces by shooting a bigbore full-auto rifle one-handed, but Gary Manning was a superb rifle marksman and strong as a young ox. He kept the FAL steady and triggered smooth, controlled, three-round bursts at the terrorists.

"Nice to have friends," McCarter rasped as he descended the ladder to the roof of the factory.

The British ace unslung his KG-99 and headed for a garret for cover. The door to the attic story opened and two armed New Guard terrorists appeared at the threshold. McCarter fired his machine pistol as he ran toward them. One killer dropped his weapon and collapsed. The other terrorist, a female New Guard, tried to pull the door shut, but the corpse of her comrade jammed the door.

McCarter fired another burst of KG-99 rounds at the door. Bullets ricocheted against the red brick door casing of the garret. Others punched into the door. At least one sizzled through the opening. The British ace heard the woman scream as a bullet struck home. He had encountered female terrorists before, and he had been forced to kill them on more than one occasion. It still made his flesh crawl to have to kill a woman, even in self-defense. Since he knew that female terrorists were as dangerous as their male counterparts—perhaps even more so, because they could appeal more to a man's tender feelings and then turn on him—they had to be dealt with the same way, and no special treatment.

"Equal opportunity," McCarter rasped through clenched teeth as he pulled the pin from an SAS "flash-bang" grenade and lobbed it through the opening.

Alarmed voices cried out from the stairwell within the attic story. The grenade exploded. The concussion blast sent a shock wave along the roof beneath McCarter's feet. A soft moan was the only sound uttered from the terrorists inside the attic stairwell.

Yakov Katzenelenbogen descended the rope ladder to the roof. Despite his artificial arm, the Israeli climbed down the rungs swiftly and hopped down from the last five feet to the rooftop. Katz immediately unslung his Uzi subgun and headed toward the garret while Gary Manning made his descent down the ladder. Soldiers in the Lan-Lung cabin fired at the terrorists to keep them occupied as the Canadian climbed to the factory roof.

Automatic fire snarled from the decks of the junk. Bullets whined along the brick cornice of the roof. Chips spewed from the edge of the roof and pelted Manning's legs as the Canadian ran for the garret. The Lan-Lung swung about and sprayed the boat with twin bursts of machine-gun fire. Bullets splintered the handrail and tore into the high poop deck of the junk. At least one terrorist was hit and toppled over the rail into the Yellow Sea.

The gunship fired another salvo of machine-gun rounds at the metal shop and the bins while a Chinese paratrooper descended the rope ladder to the factory roof. The soldier climbed the rungs to the bottom as another trooper lowered himself from the cabin of the Lan-Lung to follow. Terrorist rifle fire blasted three rounds into the second paratrooper before he could attempt to climb onto the ladder. The soldier screamed and lost his grip to plunge to the hard rooftop below. The sickening crunch of bones caused the other paratrooper to recoil from his comrade's body. After a last twitch, the dead man's sightless eyes stared fixedly at the startled trooper.

"Get over here!" Manning shouted at the paratrooper and motioned to him encouragingly. "Hurry, man! Move!"

"*Dong xun shu!*" McCarter repeated the order in Chinese. "*Lai xun shu!*"

The paratrooper rushed to the garret and joined the three Phoenix commandos as the Lan-Lung chopper rose to the sky. The plan of attack had originally called for more to get off the craft and descend to the roof, but it was previously agreed to use an alternate tactic if this proved too dangerous. The copter turned and fired a rocket. It streaked across the pier like a miniature comet, a long tail of white smoke extending behind the missile. The projectile crashed into the junk and exploded the hull near the tail mast. The vessel burst open and water gushed into the great hole. The injured and the dead tumbled from the junk into the sea, and others jumped off, either leaping to the pier or diving into the water.

"THAT'S IT, GUYS!" Calvin James exclaimed as he watched the boat begin to sink. "Time to rock and roll!"

"Music to my ears," Rafael Encizo agreed. The Cuban gathered up his MP-5 machine pistol as the patrol boat raced across the waves toward the pier.

James, Encizo and John Trent had also been flown by helicopter from their previous station along the Great Wall of China. They had not seen any action at the Wall, but they knew about the battle at the watchtower near Beijing and heard of the innocent victims. The two Phoenix Force veterans and their American ninja ally had been delivered by chopper to a patrol boat in the Yellow Sea. They were ready for combat as the boat powered through the water for the factory stronghold.

Half a dozen Chinese commandos accompanied them. Members of the newly formed *Hai Mao* Squad—which translated to "Sea Cats"—the troops were elite warriors of the People's Republic Navy. Similar in function to the U.S. SEALs, trained in Sea, Air and Land combat, the Cats seemed eager to get their claws into the terrorists. They were armed to the teeth with assault weapons, side arms, grenades and fighting knives.

Calvin James and Encizo wore black camie uniforms, boots and weaponry. James carried his trusted M-16 assault rifle with a M-203 grenade launcher attached to the underside of the barrel. He wore the Jackass Leather holster rig with the Beretta pistol under one arm and the G-96 combat dagger under the other. Encizo had his MP-5 as well as the H&K P-9S autoloader and a Cold Steel Tanto knife in a belt sheath. Another knife, a Gerber Mark I dagger, was clipped to a sheath in his boot.

Trent was once again clad in traditional ninja garb, armed with his sword and other weapons of the *ninjutsu* arsenal. In addition he carried the Ruger P-85 in shoulder leather and a Remington pump shotgun. Trent pulled up the scarf-mask to cover his mouth and nose as the boat approached its destination.

"I hope this works," Trent commented in a troubled voice.

"Don't worry," James assured him, surprised that Trent seemed concerned. "We'll kick their asses, man."

"I don't mean the raid," Trent explained. "I'm just worried about getting out of this alive and finding out I've still got trouble with the IRS when I get back home."

"We'll take care of that, too," James said with a grin.

As the boat closed in, a gunner opened fire with a mounted machine gun. More full-auto rounds hammered the wrecked hull of the sinking junk. The Lan-Lung chopper also sprayed the first-story windows of the factory building with machine-gun fire. The aircraft swung away from the building and circled around in front of the factory to cover the area while the boat pulled up to the pier.

James jumped from the boat first and climbed onto the wooden walkway. He swung his M-16 toward the metal-shop section and triggered the M-203 launcher. A 40 mm grenade belched from the big muzzle of the attachment, the recoil riding through the frame of the M-16 with considerable force. James felt the familiar buck of the plastic butt stock on his hip as he saw the grenade burst into the target. The explosion blasted a hole in the wall behind the bins. The bodies of terrorist gunmen were hurled from the cover behind the containers. The bloodied corpses fell to earth, unsightly evidence of the power of the high explosives against human flesh and bone.

Two terrorists poked their weapons around some piled-up barrels on the pier. They had made their escape from the junk before it started to sink and rushed for cover from the Lan-Lung gunship. The pair had not spotted the patrol boat until it reached the pier, and then they had hesitated a moment before taking action. That was long enough for

James to fire a grenade into the metal shop. The terrorist pair decided to take out the tall black man before he opened fire on their position with his terrifying explosive shells.

Rafael Encizo saw the enemy weapons appear over by the barrels. He swiftly sprayed the position with a volley of 9 mm parabellums. Bullets hammered the tin containers and bowled over two empty barrels stacked atop heavy, full kegs. One man tumbled from cover, both hands clasped to his bullet-smashed face. The other gunman ducked low as a barrel rolled across his arched back.

The terrorist waited for the roar of automatic fire to subside. He felt the rush of air currents, heated by the multiple high-velocity projectiles above his cowed head. The New Guard follower swung his T-56 rifle around the edge of a barrel. Encizo triggered his MP-5 and pumped two more parabellum rounds through the gunman's forehead.

More terrorists popped up along a column of sandbags between the pier and the metal shop. James swung his M-16 toward the pair and opened fire. One opponent caught three 5.56 mm slugs in the center of the chest before he could fire his T-56 blaster. The other dived for shelter behind the bags as James raked the column with a fresh burst of M-16 rounds. Sand leaked from the bags and dribbled over the terrorist's prone form. He started to crawl to a new position.

A shadow suddenly fell across the unnerved man, and he glanced up to see the sinister-looking figure of a Japanese ninja perched on the top of the sandbags. John Trent pointed his Remington shotgun at the terrorist and squeezed the trigger. A twelve-gauge burst of number four shot smashed the man's skull into a grisly ooze of blood, brains and bone fragments. Trent jumped down from the bags and jacked the pump-action of his Remington. The spent shell casing hopped from the port and another cartridge slid into the chamber.

The six *Hai Mao* commandos also dashed onto the pier, scanning the area for terrorists as they jogged for cover. Just then a terrorist hoisted himself onto the pier, his body drenched, water dripping from his clothes. He had lost his weapon when he dived from the junk, but the Sea Cat warrior who spotted the wet fanatic failed to notice this as he turned and fired a burst of T-50 slugs into the terrorist's torso. The man screamed and fell off the edge of the pier. He would not rise from the Yellow Sea a second time.

A terrorist stepped onto the overhanging stem of the sinking junk, a British Sterling subgun in his fist. He triggered a burst of 9 mm slugs and blasted the commando with a lethal dose of parabellums. Two other *Hai Mao* troops promptly returned fire and swept the terrorist off the stem of the boat with twin salvos of 7.62 mm rounds. The gunman's body splashed into the sea as another figure aboard the sinking vessel tried to dodge behind the poop, which was already partially submerged.

The two Sea Cat warriors pulled pins from grenades and hurled the explosive eggs at the crippled junk. The grenades blew up with double-power force. The boat was torn apart by the blasts, and the exposed portion burst into kindling across the waters and part of the deck. A chunk of shattered hull landed near Encizo's feet. The Cuban glanced over his shoulder at the wreckage of the destroyed vessel.

"Now, that's what I call a junk," he muttered with graveyard humor as he followed James.

The black tough guy from Chicago ran toward the main building of the factory. He ducked behind a deuce-and-a-half truck just in time to avoid a salvo of automatic fire. James cursed through clenched teeth as he opened a pouch on his belt and fished out a 40 mm cartridge-style grenade.

Encizo joined him behind the vehicle as James loaded the shell into the breech of his M-203.

James eased the M-16 around the edge of the truck and triggered the grenade launcher. The missile hurtled into the factory and struck a wall between a door and a window. The explosion tore the door from its frame and shattered the glass from the windowpane. James immediately dashed for the opening while Encizo yanked the pin from a hand grenade and lobbed it through a gaping second-story window.

The Cuban raised his MP-5 and fired a quick volley at the upstairs windows to discourage anyone within from trying to toss the grenade back outside. James charged through the ragged doorway and entered the factory, his M-16 ablaze the instant he spotted three dazed opponents. One terrorist fell lifeless to the concrete floor of a bay section. Another dropped to all fours, his T-50 chopper clattering on the floor as he hugged his bullet-torn belly with both hands.

The third man had suffered a broken shoulder from a chunk of brick propelled by the M-203 grenade blast. He held a T-56 rifle in one hand and tried to brace it against a hip as he attempted to point the weapon at James. Encizo caught sight of the injured gunman as he entered the threshold. The Cuban fired his MP-5 and nailed the terrorist with the last two rounds from the subgun magazine. The gunman toppled backward and triggered his assault rifle in a final, dying effort to fight back. His weapon blazed fiercely, but only served to blast several useless slugs into the ceiling.

The Phoenix pair ducked behind the metal frame of a box-shaped carving machine, once used to slice fish into pieces for the conveyor belt that extended across the bay area. They swapped magazines for their weapons and reloaded the M-16 and MP-5 machine pistol.

John Trent slipped inside the factory. A pistol shot bellowed within the confines of the bay section. The American ninja dived to the floor and rolled to the cutting machine. He grunted with pain as the hilt of the sword in the sash at his waist jammed under his ribs. Trent managed to hold on to his shotgun.

The ninja quickly pointed the Remington in the general direction he thought the shots had issued from. The shotgun roared, and the muzzle-flash of Trent's weapon illuminated the conveyers and machinery within the dimly lit bay. He heard the plinking noise of buckshot on metal. Another pistol shot announced the failure of the shotgun blast to strike the hidden gunman. A bullet rang against the corner of the metal frame of the cutting device, scant inches above Trent's head. The ninja ducked back to cover and pumped the action of his Remington.

"You ought to learn to handle a full-auto weapon, man," James commented as he began to creep along the length of the shelter.

"I don't do this sort of thing for a living, you know," Trent replied, taking an egg-shaped *metsubushi* from an inner pocket of his ninja costume. "Most of the time I just teach self-defense classes."

"Yeah, yeah," James muttered and peered around the edge. Two figures moved among the shadows about fifty feet from their position. "We got more of the Mao mothers on this side."

"How many?" Encizo asked, working the bolt to his MP-5.

"Not sure," the black commando admitted. "Hard to say in the dark. The guys on this side are trying to creep up on us. They're holding their fire. Must figure we don't know they're there."

"Let 'em feel confident for now," Encizo stated. The Cuban noticed Trent had a ninja "sight-remover" in his fist. "Good idea, John. We don't want to use any frag or concussion grenades in here or we'll take the chance of eating some shrapnel ourselves. Lob that thing at the pistol-packer by the conveyors. Cal, you ready for the bastards on your side?"

"Naw, I decided to take a nap, man," James replied tensely. "Give me a little credit. Do it, jack."

Trent hurled the *metsubushi*. It sailed across the bay section and struck a wall. The flash powder and pepper burst on impact. A terrorist cried out as pepper flew into his eyes. The glare of the flash powder illuminated the figure as he pawed at his face with one hand and waved a T-51 autoloader in the other. Another terrorist was crouched by a conveyor belt, his head bowed and eyes squeezed shut to try to guard them from the bright light. The T-50 subgun in his fists was pointed toward the Phoenix team's position.

Encizo swung his MP-5 at the man with the Chinese chopper and Trent pointed his Remington at the terrorist affected by the pepper. The Cuban pumped a three-round burst into the bowed head of his target. The gunman's skull exploded, and the instant corpse collapsed on the floor. Trent's shotgun spit again, and a blast of buckshot smashed into the chest of the other New Guard devotee. The impact hurled the bloodied figure against a concrete wall.

The two terrorists James had noticed made their move and rushed the defenders' position. The Phoenix fighter from Chicago was ready for them. His M-16 spit flame and drilled three projectiles upward through the solar plexus of one opponent. James swung his rifle toward the other terrorist. As the man dived to the floor and tried to roll for safety, James tracked the movement and fired three more bullets into the tumbling shape. The terrorist came to a dead halt.

AN SAS FLASH-BANG GRENADE exploded in the second-story office section. The blast stunned five New Guard triggermen and a pair of European mercenaries. Some of the terrorists fired blindly as David McCarter streaked through the doorway in a low position. His KG-99 fired a merciless salvo of 9 mm parabellums into the body of the closest opponent.

The Chinese fanatic fell like a side of beef while a French mercenary triggered a .45 Colt pistol at the British commando. The big 230-grain slug punched into a wall just to the right of McCarter. The Phoenix pro barely flinched, and promptly returned fire with his KG-99 machine pistol. The Frenchman was driven by the force of three flat-nose parabellums, then after toppling over a tabletop he folded up on the floor.

Two other New Guards were about to swing their weapons toward McCarter as Yakov Katzenelenbogen entered the room. The Israeli's Uzi subgun slashed a deadly diagonal column of full-auto 115-grain NATO 9 mm rounds across the upper torso of one gunman and caught the other opponent in the face.

A German merc had ducked under a table when the shooting began. He rose swiftly and pitched the furniture into David McCarter while the Briton's attention was on another opponent. The table crashed into McCarter and knocked him to the floor. The machine pistol slid away from the British commando's fingers.

Katz dropped to one knee as the German gunman triggered an American-made M-3A1 "grease gun." The submachine gun roared and a column of .45-caliber slugs ripped into the wall above the Israeli's head. Katz returned fire with the Uzi. Bullets tore under the soft tissue of the hollow of the German's jawbone, then plowed upward into his brain.

The second European killer collapsed as the last Asian terrorist in the quarters raised a T-51 autoloader and pointed it at Katz. McCarter pushed aside the table, Browning Hi-Power already in his fist. The Briton snap-aimed and fired the familiar handgun. A well-placed round struck the gunman in the face. Blood gushed from a punctured eye socket as the bullet burned a lethal pathway. The back of the terrorist's head mushroomed into a spray of brain tissue and blood when the parabellum burst open a nasty exit wound.

"You okay, David?" Katz inquired, glancing about the room to be certain the battle was over—for the moment.

"A bit ruffled is all," the Briton assured him, retrieving his KG-99.

Gary Manning glanced inside the office section and saw that his partners were unharmed. The Canadian continued along the corridor with a Chinese paratrooper to check the other rooms on the second story. The doors to most of the rooms stood open with no occupants within, but they were drawing close to a closed door. The trooper prepared to slam it open with his boot, but Manning placed a hand on his shoulder and shook his head. The Asian soldier nodded and looked at him questioningly.

The Phoenix Force demolitions expert unslung the pack from his back and opened a canvas compartment to remove a small glob of gray putty substance. Manning had devised the special plastic explosive himself. It included a buffer element to reduce the force of the blast for occasions when a powerful explosion was neither necessary nor safe. He fastened the jell to the doors by the handle and inserted a pencil detonator.

The paratrooper watched Manning attentively, fascinated by the Canadian's skill. He failed to notice the muzzle of a T-56 rifle at the corner of the doorway up the hall. The terrorist gunman opened fire and four 7.62 mm slugs crashed into the paratrooper's torso. The Asian was thrown to the floor as Manning swiftly swung his FAL toward the muzzle-flash of the assassin's weapon. He triggered a short burst. Three bullets plowed into the terrorist's right biceps and shoulder.

The impact of the multiple projectiles yanked the man off balance and sent him staggering across the threshold. He still held on to his T-56 rifle, although it was doubtful he could have fired the weapon. But Manning could not afford to take any chances, and dispatched a trio of FAL rounds to the chest. The gunman tumbled down the corridor and fell in a twitching heap.

Another figure emerged from the room with his hands held at shoulder-level. Manning nearly fired on the man before he realized the terrorist was unarmed. The Canadian kept his finger on the trigger and kept the man covered as he slowly stepped from the room.

"Keep your hands up!" Manning shouted. "Make a quick move and you're dead!"

The terrorist's hands trembled slightly as he stepped into the hallway. But he turned in a slight giveaway motion and Manning realized there must be another opponent in the room. It was a setup of some kind.

A pistol snarled. The terrorist's head recoiled violently as a 7.65 mm round punched a hole in his forehead. The man collapsed dead on the floor. A T-51 pistol landed on the chest of the corpse. A Type 50 submachine gun was tossed through the doorway and clattered next to the lifeless shape.

"Don't shoot!" a voice called out in flawless English. "I'm unarmed!"

"Move real slow!" Manning instructed, rifle held ready. "If I have any reason to suspect a trick, I'll take you out quicker than you killed that other bastard!"

Ming Ssu slowly emerged from the room, hands held high in surrender. Katz and McCarter stepped into the corridor as the ex-SAD agent appeared. The Israeli helped Manning cover Ming while McCarter knelt beside the body of the slain paratrooper to vainly search for signs of life. Ming raised an eyebrow with surprise when he saw none of his captors were Chinese.

"Apparently CIA is cooperating with the Social Affairs Department these days," Ming remarked. "Things have certainly changed since I was in the business."

"Ming Ssu, I presume?" Katz commented.

"You know who I am?" The renegade was again surprised. "You people must be pretty good. Well, you won. So, let's talk about a deal, gentlemen."

"I wouldn't count on it, Ming," Katz replied in a flat, hard voice.

17

"Man, we're in big-time shit," Paul Gowers rasped as he gripped the M-16 assault rifle in his small white hands.

"We don't need a status report, idiot," Craig Kelly growled in reply. The big black dope pusher turned to Carlton Neville. "You're supposed to be the unit genius. What do we do now?"

The British mercenary closed his eyes and leaned his forehead against the plastic forestock of his M-16 as he squatted behind the row of rotted old wooden pallets stacked near a wall in a bay area. Jesus wept, Neville thought as he tried to come up with some choice of action that offered some chance of survival. The attack on the base had happened so quickly, so professionally. The factory had been hit from all sides. The opponent was well armed, obviously well trained and far better organized than Commander Kuo Chun's people. They were chopping through the People's New Guard like wheat at harvest time.

"All right," Neville began in a low whisper. "We can't hide here forever. If they catch us, it'll mean a firing squad for certain. I think that's how they execute chaps these days in China. We have to make a break for freedom. I reckon our best chance is to head for the rear."

"There's been a hell of a lot of shootin' and explosions going off in that direction, Neville," Gowers reminded him. "We could run right into a hundred troops."

"They've probably taken out all the New Guard sheep at the rear of the building and on the pier," Neville insisted. "It's our best chance."

"Hey, they blasted the ship but good," Kelly stated. "What the fuck good is it gonna do if we do get out of here? We ain't gonna jump in the water and swim for South Korea."

"No," Neville agreed. "We'll jump into the water and swim under the pier. We hold on to the supports and just wait for the bastards to pull out. With a bit of luck, they won't think to check under the pier, and we can climb out after they leave."

Gowers groaned. "That idea sucks."

"Unless you can think of something better," Kelly growled, "shut up. Okay, Neville. Let's go for it."

The trio of renegades moved around the row of pallets. Gowers stepped around the corner of the stacked pallets, rifle held in front of him. Neville and Kelly followed. Gowers eased his M-16 barrel around the edge of the shelter.

The barrel of another M-16, complete with M-203 attachment, appeared from behind the brick pillar of a ceiling support. Gowers saw the threat too late. A three-round burst slammed into his chest. He fell backward against Neville. The force of the falling body knocked the rifle from the British mercenary's grasp. Neville jumped back and reached for the .45 Colt on his hip. Kelly cursed as he ducked low behind the pallets, his assault rifle clenched tightly to his barrel chest.

"Son of a Siamese bitch," Kelly rasped, glancing down at Gowers's bullet-ravaged corpse. "Paul got through Nam without a scratch..."

"His problems are over," Neville said sharply, without a trace of sympathy. "Ours aren't. I spotted a grenade launcher on the weapon that took out Gowers. The bastard could blow us to hell and there's nothing we can do about it."

"Hey, you losers!" Calvin James's voice called from the pillar. "I got a good enough look at you trash to know you're heroin-pushing scum bags with major league yellow stripes down your back! I want you rat droppings to know a Vietnam veteran—a *real* Vietnam vet—is gonna smoke your ass!"

Neville thrust his Colt pistol into his belt at the small of his back. He gestured for Kelly to toss his rifle. The black renegade replied with a rigid middle-finger salute as he mouthed a silent obscenity that told Neville to do something that was biologically impossible.

"Look, that Yank sounds like one of those Boy Scout, hero sorts who believes in all that code-of-honor rot," Neville hissed. "Not the sort to shoot an unarmed opponent."

"You gonna bet your life on that?" Kelly demanded. "Go ahead, but I ain't takin' that gamble."

"Hide the .45, same as I've done," the Briton insisted. "If we can catch him off guard there's still a chance. Otherwise, he'll fire that launcher. What do you think your chances are then?"

Neville raised his hands and stepped from the pallets. Kelly reluctantly tossed out his M-16 and followed. The black thug stuck his Colt pistol into his belt out of view before he walked out with his hands raised. James saw the pair and began to squeeze the trigger of his rifle. The Phoenix fighter held his fire, a little bit surprised that the opponents had decided to surrender.

"Don't shoot!" Neville urged. "I wasn't in Vietnam! You got me wrong, fella! In fact I've infiltrated this gang of bandits as part of a mission for Interpol."

"Kiss my ass," James barked, slowly moving from cover, weapon pointed at the pair. "Save the fairy tales for your cell mates when you have trouble going to sleep in whatever prison you wind up in."

"Chill out, bro," Kelly said with a nervous smile.

"You call me that again, I'll shoot your balls off," James warned, his voice as hard as tempered steel. "No son of a bitch who deserts his buddies and sells dope is a brother of mine. I don't give a shit what color he is."

James glanced at the pallets, suspicious of a trick. He had only seen two opponents when he opened fire on Gowers, but there were three total. Maybe a fourth lurked behind the barrier. Neville and Kelly slowly advanced, hands at shoulder level.

"Far enough!" James snapped. "Hit the deck! Arms extended in front of you with the palms turned up!"

"All right," Neville replied as he bent his knees and slowly lowered his body. "Take it easy..."

His hand streaked for the pistol at the small of his back as he dived for the ground. The British merc drew the Colt and assumed a prone stance. Kelly followed his example a fragment of a second later. The big black man's hand closed on the grips of his pistol as Calvin James opened fire.

Carlton Neville's face exploded into a grisly pulp. Three 5.56 mm slugs had smashed it beyond recognition. Kelly gasped in alarm and terror as James swung the M-16 toward him. The renegade tossed away the .45 and thrust his arms overhead. Kelly sat on his knees, hands raised and eyes wide with fear. James trained the assault rifle on the gangster's face as he stepped closer.

"There are guns lying on the floor," James declared, his eyes ablaze with anger. "Go ahead and grab one."

"No way, bro," Kelly declared with a sneer. "You wanna kill me? I ain't givin' you no excuses!"

James lowered the rifle barrel. The muzzle hovered inches from Kelly's forehead. The renegade shook with fear. Kelly closed his eyes tight and clenched his teeth as beads of cold sweat covered his ebony features. James's finger rested on the trigger of his M-16. Part of Calvin James wanted to put a bullet in the traitor's brain. It would be easy, but living with himself after he committed cold-blooded murder would not be.

"Aw, hell," James muttered and lashed a kick to Kelly's face.

His heel slammed into the traitor's jaw. Kelly fell backward to the floor in a dazed lump. James kicked the renegade in the ribs and pushed with the stock of his rifle to roll Kelly on to his belly. The Phoenix pro planted a knee between Kelly's shoulder blades and reached for some unbreakable plastic riot cuffs in his belt.

"If things were the other way around, you wouldn't have minded killing me," James commented to the unconscious opponent as he bound Kelly's wrists together. "But I'm different from you. Thank God."

RAFAEL ENCIZO and John Trent approached a corridor that branched off from the bay sections. A New Guard terrorist thrust a T-50 subgun around the archway of the corridor and aimed the weapon at the Cuban and his ninja companion. Encizo's MP-5 and Trent's shotgun roared before the enemy gunman could open fire. Parabellum slugs and buckshot tore into the terrorist. The corpse flopped onto the floor, virtually decapitated and oozing crimson from a dozen wounds.

Encizo rushed to the archway and peered around the corner. Half a dozen terrorists fled down the hallway to a room at the end of the corridor. A female fanatic turned and pointed a pistol at Encizo as she ran. The Cuban blasted away with a trio of H&K full-auto slugs. She flew against a startled male comrade who shoved her aside as he followed the others to the doorway of the room.

Trent joined Encizo at the mouth of the corridor. The Cuban gestured for Trent to stay put as he drew a concussion grenade from his belt. Encizo hurled the blaster at the open door down the hall. He and Trent ducked back to the archway and waited half a second. The grenade exploded with a monstrous bellow.

"Let's go," Encizo announced as he bolted into the corridor.

The ninja followed, pumping his Remington as he ran. The pair charged into the room at the end of the hall. It was the *kwoon* martial arts training gym. Four terrorists had been knocked to the hardwood floor by the concussion blast. One opponent was staggering around unsteadily, a T-56 rifle in his fists.

"*Diào bù giang!*" Trent snapped, his Remington shotgun pointed at the terrorist still on his feet. From the threatening look in the ninja's eyes it was easy to understand what he meant even without words.

The fanatic chose to ignore the order or perhaps he did not hear it due to the ringing in his ears caused by the concussion blast directly outside the *kwoon*. Either way, he did not drop his rifle. Trent triggered the shotgun. A dull click was the only response. He had exhausted the tubular magazine supply of shells.

Encizo opened fire. His MP-5 let loose a trio of high-velocity messengers into the gunman's upper torso. The terrorist struck the floor with a liquid slap. The bloodied corpse lay near the other terrorists as they slowly raised their heads to face Encizo and the black-clad ninja.

"Tell them to get their hands up," Encizo said to Trent, his H&K blaster pointed at the four dazed figures. "Tell them if one man pulls a weapon we'll kill them all."

Trent lowered the empty shotgun to the floor and drew his Ruger P-85 autoloader from shoulder leather. He had just started to translate the instructions into Mandarin Chinese when another door opened at the other side of the *kwoon*. A man with a T-50 submachine gun appeared at the entrance. Trent immediately swung his pistol toward the new threat and triggered two shots. Both 9 mm slugs found their target, and the gunman slumped against the doorway, the unfired subgun still in his fists.

The four terrorists on the floor reacted as if the shots were a signal to attack. Encizo's MP-5 erupted and emptied its last two rounds into the closest opponent. Another of the New Guard swung a fist with a bayonet in it. Encizo gripped the empty MP-5 in one fist and raised it to block the blade with the steel frame of the machine pistol. Sharp metal clanged against the H&K blaster.

With his free hand Encizo drew his Cold Steel Tanto from the belt sheath in a fast, smooth motion. The Cuban's arm shot forward before his opponent could attempt another attack. The six-inch steel blade of the Tanto knife plunged into the hollow of the terrorist's throat. Encizo twisted his wrist and yanked the blade free. A torrent of blood gushed from the wound and poured across the Asian extremist's shirtfront. The man dropped his bayonet and stumbled backward, his hands gripped around his bleeding neck. His knees folded and he wilted to the floor.

The barrel of a T-56 rifle chopped Trent's forearm and struck the Ruger P-85 from the American ninja's fingers. Trent swiftly snap-kicked his opponent between the legs and seized the frame of the T-56. He shoved hard and drove the butt stock of the rifle into its owner's chest. The blow propelled the terrorist backward into the path of the fourth New Guard psycho.

Trent held on to his opponent's rifle with one hand, pushing the barrel toward the ceiling. His other hand slashed a "tiger claw" stroke at the terrorist's face. The tips and nails of arched fingers raked the fanatic's eyes. The man screamed and released the T-56 to clasp his torn eyeballs. Blood trickled between his fingers. Trent thrust a "panther punch" under the injured man's chin. The second row of bent knuckles struck with terrible force. The ruthless stroke crushed the terrorist's thyroid cartilage and caved in his windpipe.

The remaining New Guard follower managed to keep his balance and tried to aim his T-51 autoloader at Trent. Encizo's arm snapped forward like the tail of a scorpion and let the Tanto fly. The Cold Steel knife was not designed for throwing, but Encizo was an expert with a blade and adept at accurately throwing knives—even those not properly balanced for the task.

The point of the Tanto struck the terrorist in the sternum. The heavy blade split bone and lodged in the man's chest. He reeled, pistol in his fist, but his attention was centered on the horrible pain and the terrifying sight of the big Cold Steel knife jammed in his flesh. Encizo lashed out a boot and kicked the T-51 from the terrorist's hand before he could recover his wits and open fire.

The terrorist crumpled to the floor beside his dying colleague. Trent reached for his fallen pistol and Encizo prepared to reload his MP-5. Their attention was drawn by the brazen arrival of another man at the doorway. The Cuban yanked his H&K P-9S pistol from leather and pointed it at the muscular young man who stepped boldly into the room.

Chien strode proudly forward, hand placed on the hilt of the sword thrust into his sash. The Maoist commando glared at Encizo as if daring him to pull the trigger. Trent left the Ruger pistol on the floor and stepped toward Chien. Encizo held his fire, but clucked his tongue with dismay.

"You don't have to do it, John," the Cuban declared, well aware of what Trent intended.

"He isn't going to surrender," Trent replied, his eyes fixed on the Chinese swordsman. "You can see that by his manner and his expression. He is prepared to die and to test his skills one last time."

"Why the hell should he get what he wants?" Encizo snorted.

"Because I can give it to him," Trent answered, watching Chien draw closer. "And because the challenge of a sword duel is a lure I can't resist any more than he can."

"You might try a little harder," Encizo complained.

Trent and Chien faced each other near the center of the room. Racks of traditional Chinese martial arts weapons lined the walls. The flag of the People's Republic of China was mounted on a wall next to a large painting of Chairman Mao. Trent glanced at the picture and suddenly dipped a hand inside his *gi* jacket.

Chien arched his back, prepared to weave or duck if Trent hurled a weapon. The Chinese killer was familiar with the legends of ninja warriors. He realized their fighting style was unorthodox and ruthless. However, Trent's arm snapped toward the painting of the Chairman. A star-shaped *shaken* struck the likeness of Mao Tse-tung, and sharp tines stuck in the forehead of the late tyrant's picture.

Chien howled with rage at this insult to the man he worshiped as a god. He drew his long, double-edged sword and attacked. Trent's *ninja-do* hissed from its scabbard and rose to block his opponent's weapon. Blades clashed. Chien did not lose his self-control, but channeled his anger into his attack. He pushed with his sword stroke, his entire body moving with the blow. The force drove Trent backward.

The Maoist fanatic delivered a quick thrust. His sword was better suited for stabbing than Trent's ninja blade. Trent dodged the thrust and parried Chien's sword with his own. He pivoted, spun to the right of Chien and delivered an overhead stroke. Chien's blade whipped upward and deflected the attack. The Chinese swordsman swung a cross-body cut to Trent's belly.

Encizo sucked air through clenched teeth as he saw Trent recoil from the blow. A streak of crimson appeared on the ninja's black *gi* at stomach-level. Chien swung his sword overhead for another stroke aimed at Trent's head. The American ninja raised his sword like a bar, one fist around the handle and the other hand braced on the unsharpened edge of the blade. Chien's sword rang against steel once again.

Trent lashed a hook-kick under Chien's ribs. The Maoist gasped from the unexpected blow and Trent shoved his opponent's blade away. Chien jumped out of range of Trent's weapon before the ninja could follow the move with another attack. Both men squared off once more, their swords held ready, ready to skewer the opponent.

Chien delivered a short thrust, a feint. He altered the attack to a fast roundhouse stroke, intended to decapitate Trent. The ninja was not fooled by the false thrust. Trent parried his opponent's sword with the flat of his own blade. Suddenly Trent stepped forward and snapped both arms upward in a quick uppercut stroke.

The butt of his sword handle slammed into Chien's fists. The force of the blow sent the Chinese sword flying from its owner's fingers. Trent's sword descended in a diagonal slash that sliced Chien from collarbone to sternum. Blood squirted from the long, deep wound as Chien staggered backward, mouth open in a mute cry of mortal agony.

Trent delivered a fast thrust and plunged the tip of his *ninja-do* into Chien's chest. The sharp steel sunk into the Chinese killer's heart. Chien stared at Trent with astonishment as he sagged toward the floor. Trent planted a foot on his opponent and yanked the sword from the man's lifeless flesh. Chien's corpse sprawled at the ninja's feet.

Calvin James whistled softly as he entered the *kwoon* and found it littered with numerous dead bodies. "Hell! You guys sure made a mess in here."

"The maid service can send us a bill," Encizo replied dryly. "John got wounded. Sword cut to the abdomen."

"I'll take a look at it," James said, approaching the ninja and taking his medic kit from his belt.

"It's not that bad really," Trent assured him, returning his sword to its scabbard. "I've been cut worse. Speaking of cuts—can you people handle any sort of tax reduction for this year's income...?"

THE BATTLE WAS OVER. The shooting and the explosions had ceased. The majority of the People's New Guard had been killed during the raid. Ming Ssu, Craig Kelly and a few lesser-ranking members of the terrorist outfit had been taken alive. Chinese paratroopers and *Hai Mao* commandos helped round up the survivors as the Lan-Lung gunship landed on the pier.

David McCarter peered from a second-story window of the factory building. He saw the big rotor blades of the helicopter below. As men emerged from the aircraft and moved to the building, another copter appeared in the sky and approached the site. McCarter turned to Yakov Katzenelenbogen.

"Our ride is here," he announced. "Better get ready to go."

"Yes," Katz replied, not looking at McCarter. "It's all over now. The SAD and the Chinese government will still have to take care of a few loose ends, but we're certainly finished here."

He stared down at Commander Kuo Chun. Katz and McCarter had found the terrorist leader in a small room on the second story. Kuo's duffel bag was open. Her few belongings had been removed, and the framed pictures of Chairman Mao and her parents were propped against a wall next to her still figure.

Kuo lay on her back, her legs folded under her in a manner that would have been extremely uncomfortable if she were alive. The T-51 pistol was still clenched in her fist. A crimson hole in her right temple confirmed the method used by Kuo to take her own life. Katz glanced at the pictures of the three individuals who had created Kuo Chun. They had probably been the only people Kuo had ever loved or truly cared about. Their faces appeared to have been the last thing on earth Kuo beheld before she killed herself.

Had she devoted all her energy, time and intellect to an obsessive effort to somehow get the approval of her dead father and mother and a politician who had written a little red book that became her holy scriptures? How many other Red Guard extremists were like Kuo Chun, brainwashed by an extensive government program of concentrated Maoism until it became engraved into mind and spirit? How many fanatics of other philosophies in other countries were plotting destructive actions that would only end in tragedy and death? The Phoenix leader wondered how many others would throw their lives away and cause the death of countless others due to the dogma of madness?

"What a waste," Katz said, shaking his head sadly. "All right, David. Let's be off."

Nui Ba Den. Charlie holds the mountain stronghold until Special Forces takes it back.

VIETNAM: GROUND ZERO.

STRIKE

ERIC HELM

An elite Special Forces team is dispatched when heavy traffic in enemy supplies to Nui Ba Den has intelligence in Saigon worried. Primed for action, Mack Gerber and his men wage a firefight deep inside a mountain fortress, while the VC outside are poised for a suicide raid against an American political delegation.

Mack Bolan's

PHOENIX FORCE

by Gar Wilson

The battle-hardened, five-man commando unit known as Phoenix Force continues its onslaught against the hard realities of global terrorism in an endless crusade for freedom, justice and the rights of the individual. Schooled in guerrilla warfare, equipped with the latest in lethal weapons, Phoenix Force's adventures have made them a legend in their own time. Phoenix Force is the free world's foreign legion!

"Gar Wilson is excellent! Raw action attacks the reader on every page."

—Don Pendleton

Phoenix Force titles are available
wherever paperbacks are sold.

PF-1

A different world—
a different war

JAMES AXLER

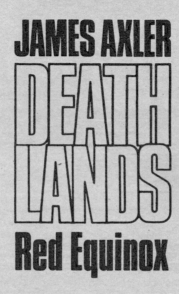

DEATH LANDS

Red Equinox

Ryan Cawdor and his band of postnuclear survivors enter a malfunctioning gateway and are transported to Moscow, where Americans are hated with an almost religious fervor and blamed for the destruction of the world.

DL-9

DON PENDLETON's
MACK BOLAN®

More SuperBolan bestseller action! Longer than the monthly series, SuperBolans feature Mack in more intricate, action-packed plots— more of a good thing